B

THE TEN O'CLOCK HORSES

LAURIE GRAHAM

THE TEN O'CLOCK HORSES

BANTAM PRESS

LONDON · NEW YORK · TORONTO · SYDNEY · AUCKLAND

TRANSWORLD PUBLISHERS LTD
61–63 Uxbridge Road, London W5 5SA

TRANSWORLD PUBLISHERS (AUSTRALIA) PTY LTD
15–25 Helles Avenue, Moorebank, NSW 2170

TRANSWORLD PUBLISHERS (NZ) LTD
3 William Pickering Drive, Albany, Auckland

Published 1996 by Bantam Press
a division of Transworld Publishers Ltd
Copyright © Laurie Graham 1996

Extracts from 'Chicago, Chicago' (H. Mancini, A. Bergman,
M. Bergman) © 1969 EMI Catalogue Partnership,
EMI U Catalogue Inc. and EMI Northridge Music Inc., USA.

A catalogue record for this book is available from the British
Library

ISBN 0593 039297

Typeset in 11/15pt Linotype Times by
Kestrel Data, Exeter, Devon.

Printed and bound in Great Britain by
Mackays of Chatham plc, Chatham, Kent.

For Isabel, Alastair, Fiona and Sinéad

THE TEN O'CLOCK HORSES

Seven fifteen, and a fresh June morning that promises well. Ronnie Glover, tiptoeing out of the Woodleigh Guest-House (Hot & Cold running water in all rooms) with a flatpack of Izal inside his windcheater and a weight on his mind. The best of the day. All that air nobody has breathed. Perfect for a gentle meander down the cliff path, past the Poop Deck (Ovaltine 1s 6d, Milkshakes 2 shillings) and the Krayzee Golf (Last tickets 6.45 p.m.) to Mick & Gina's Beachside Stores for a hot, sweet tea and a read of the *Mirror*.

What a balls-up. What a fucking balls-up. Paying three times what we'd have had to pay for a caravan, going up in the world, supposed to be, staying in a boarding-house, guest-house, and then having to slope down here every morning to do what a man's got to do. Not enough food neither. Farting little helpings. Two potatoes each. Guts rumbling all the time. I could have a breakfast before I go back for breakfast. No. Eileen'd smell it. Some holiday. Susan chewing gum. Bloody I-Spy books all over the place. Gillian scowling and answering back and going to the lav with a Dr White's

9

up the sleeve of her cardigan. And not even any whassisname on Friday. Sharing a bastard room with the chewer and the scowler, so definitely no whassisname, don't matter how quiet you promise to keep it. Quite a few out and about for not even eight o'clock. Escape squads, wriggled out under the wire. Staying at places worse than the Woodleigh. Could be. Places that haven't even got a Ludo board, never mind about having to sign for it. Look at him. He's from the Rutherglen (Dogs welcome. Vacancies). Wife wears peep-toe sandals. He's not happy. Sticks out a mile. Mooching this early, talking to anybody. Mick's got a nice little set-up though. Easter till September. Hot drinks. Ice-creams. Fishing nets and all that for the kiddies. Coining it in. Fresh air. Sea views. I could do that. Some of this lot are up so early because they go to bed so early, because once they've walked down the pier, had half of shandy and walked back, there's bugger all else to do. Play with the grapnel machine in the arcade, see if you can win a fluffy duckling. Hang about for the end of Variety Nite and try to get Yana's autograph. Chicago, Chicago, 's a wonderful town. Chicago, Chicago, I'll show you around. Ah yes. Here we go. It's an amazing thing how a drop of hot tea at the top end gets business moving along down below. The human alimentary canal is nearly thirty feet long. Or is it thirty yards? Give it a few minutes. No hurry. No strangers rattling the door, waiting right outside so you can hear them breathing. No Eileen saying, 'I hope you're not going to leave a pong in there, Ron?' Nobody alerting the bloody Press. Just a nice early morning clear-out and no holds barred.

Ronnie Glover, heading for his favourite cubicle of the Esplanade Municipal Gents' Conveniences while his family sleeps.

'Is that what I should get them, do you think?'

'What's that, darling?'

'The letter rack.'

'Could do.'

'Or the cruet?'

'Could do.'

'Ron?'

'What?'

'You're not listening to a word I'm saying.'

'I'm asleep.'

'Well somebody's got to get cracking. If somebody doesn't get cracking there won't be any presents bought for anybody. Are you listening to me?'

'I'm on holiday.'

'*I'm* on holiday. I think Ma'd like the letter rack.'

'I'm hungry.'

'You're always hungry.'

'I'm starving, Eileen. All I had last night was two jollops of coronation chicken and a scratty little slice of apple pie. And all I had this morning was two chipolatas and half a tomato.'

'You should fill up with toast.'

'I don't want to fill up with toast. I want to fill up with bacon and fried eggs. Eileen?'

'What?'

'How are we going to go on? You know? With the girls being in the same room.'

'You'll have to hang on till we get home.'

'You said that about having a shit. I can't hang on. I keep getting stiffies. Eileen. Eileen?'

'Keep your voice down.'

'I've got one now.'

'Well I expect you'll get another one when we get home. Are you coming with me?'

'Where?'

'To get a present for Ma and Pop. Are you coming with me?'

'No. I'm going to do my Italian lesson.'

'Well when Gillian turns up tell her she's to stay put till I get back. And if Susan goes in the sea make sure she puts her swimming hat on and when she comes out put some more Nivea on her shoulders. And if the deck-chair man comes round tell him we're not paying for this one because it's got a big dob of tar on it.'

'Right. Bring us a sausage roll.'

'What did you say?'

'Bring us three sausage rolls. Please.'

Lesson Four. Useful irregular verbs, Present Indicative. Potere, *to be able.* Posso, puoi, puo, possiamo, potete, possono. Volere, *to desire or want.* Voglio, vuoi, vuole, vogliamo, volete, vogliono.

Voglio imparare Italiano. Posso parlare Italiano. Vogliamo parlare Italiano. Quando il professore parla Italiano, capiamo tutto.

*   *   *

Ronnie, with a very new copy of *Italiano Vivo*, and his back to the sea, so as to have a better view of the bucket and spade shop. Gina, of Mick & Gina's Beachside Stores, hanging fresh supplies of novelty air rings beneath the awning, revealing, in little flashes and longer, innocent stretches, an aspect of woman Ronnie has never seen before, never even thought about. An aspect of woman that has made him clean forget how to conjugate *preferire*. A sweet, white armpit, filled with tiny black Italian curls.

'Oh Gina. *Ecco la matita. La matita è rossa.*'

'Come on.'

'No. I told you.'

'You can do that after.'

'And be up half the night.'

'Well I'm going.'

'You're no help, Ron. You're no flipping help at all. You leave it all to me. Booking up. Finding somebody to have the dog. All the ironing. All the packing. The presents. The postcards. And then I have all the washing when we get back. It's no holiday for me, Ron. I'm flipping fed up with it.'

'So sod the presents and bollocks to the postcards. Come on out.'

'You've not made any effort in the dining-room. If somebody says "Good Morning" or asks you to pass the sauce, you could make a bit of conversation.'

'I don't want to. I'm on holiday with my family. I don't want to pal up with some bloke from the Pru, just because he's asked me to pass the sauce.'

'Nobody's asking you to pal up. You could just say something. In English. Not pretend Italian.'

'It's not pretend Italian. All right. What am I supposed to say? I see the barometer's set fair? Read any good books lately? Tell me, do you own any sports shirts that aren't the colour of goose cack? They say we may expect rain before tea?'

*　　*　　*

Susan and Gillian, curled up on the Z-bed with a copy of *Jackie*, laughing, but very very quietly.

'Go on. Take the mickey. It's all you ever do. People just want to be ordinary, Ron. They don't want to be looking at leather settees and drawing ladies' bottoms and talking *parli italiooli*. They just want you to pass the sauce nicely and ask them something about Tamworth.'

'Tamworth?'

'And when his wife offered you a Rennie, she was only trying to help. She thought you'd got acid indigestion. She was only being pleasant.'

'Well fuck fucking Tamworth, Eileen. And the fucking Rennies. I've just about had it with this fucking holiday.'

'Keep your voice down.'

'I will not. I'll open this fucking door and invite them all to come and listen.'

'Now you're being ridiculous.'

'You're right. I'm a ridiculous man having a ridiculous fucking holiday. I work all fucking year . . .'

'Ron . . .'

'. . . So I can have two weeks getting sand in my belly button, and where am I? In some tight-arsed boarding-house . . .'

'Guest-house.'

'Some tight-arsed boarding-house, where I can't go to the bog because my shit stinks, and there's never enough grub, and the dining-room's full of wazzocks from Tamworth who think having your toast cut corner to corner is like dining at the fucking Ritz. I've got two girls answering me back and forever whispering and rinsing out their knickers. And I've got a wife who's always got too much ironing to come out and have a drink with me, and then we get here and she wants me to pal up with some God-botherers from Tamworth. And then . . .'

'Ron, you'll get us chucked out.'

'Good. And then, when I want to go for a stroll along the pier

14

and finish up at the chippy, she tells me she's too busy writing fucking bollocking postcards. You're round the bend, Eileen. Round the fucking bend. Susan, Gillian, get your cardigans. We're going out.'

Ronnie Glover, with a daughter under each arm, cosied up on a clifftop seat, listening to the sea, just down there in the dark, watching the lights of a passing frigate, thinking about Ratcliffe and Jimmy and Bonk and all the lads off HMS *Sherwood* that he didn't know the names of even though he'd heard them in the water, calling for their Mams, crying not to drown. Ronnie, being fed chips and vinegary pieces of perfect battered cod, glad to be alive.

'Are you awake? Eileen?'
    Silence.
    'We brought you something.'
    Silence.
    'Peace offering.'
    'What?'
    'Mushy peas and a pie.'
    'You can't bring food in. It's against the rules.'
    'Got you! Got you going! No. We didn't really bring you mushies. Brought you some choccy though. Want a bit?'
    'I've cleaned my teeth.'
    'So? Go on. Have a bit of choccy.'
    'Put it on the side.'
    'A little bit? A tiddly-widdly diddly bit? A slither? A sliver? Here you are. I'll shave a little shaving off it and slide it between your lips so's you'll hardly notice.'
    'Go to sleep.'
    'Friends?'
    'Yeah.'
    'Finished your postcards?'
    'Yeah. Hang your trousers up.'

15

'Can't see to hang anything up. Keep stubbing my bloody toe. It was lovely out. Just a little bit of breeze. You should have come. Dear God, who's dropped one? Susan? Is that you?'

'Dad!'

'Well it wasn't me. Was it? That's a belter. Well done that girl. Only a daughter of mine could drop one as good as that. Silent, but deadly.'

'Dad! It wasn't me.'

'Must have been your Mum then.'

'Night, Dad.'

'Night, girls. Eileen?'

'What?'

'Have you got hairy armpits?'

'Anybody home?'

Eileen Glover, carrying a Blackgang Chine letter rack, Susan Glover carrying a plastic replica of The Needles lighthouse filled with layers of different coloured sands, Ronnie with a bit of a sun-tan, Gillian with a love-bite.

'You're back then.'

Ma, welcoming her only son and his family, without missing a beat of *The Black and White Minstrel Show*.

'Hello, hello, hello.'

Pop, blanketed under the *News of the World*, perking up at the sight of Susan.

'Look what I got, Grandad.'

'Mm. That's nobby. What is it?'

'It's sand from Alum Bay. You can buy an empty lighthouse and fill it up yourself, but we didn't have enough time.'

'Mm. That's lovely. See that, Ma? All different coloured sands. And did you have a donkey ride for your old Grandad?'

'They don't have donkey rides.'

17

'No donkey rides? Whatever kind of a seaside is that? Did you dig a big hole and bury your Dad?'

'Yeah.'

'And I told her, never mind about leaving his head clear. Cover him over and pat it down flat. He's had a right old mood on him all holiday. Haven't you?'

'Has he? What's up, son?'

'Nothing that a good holiday wouldn't cure.'

'You're brown though.'

'Browned off.'

'Did you see that? That girl in the chorus nearly fell over. She went right into the girl next to her.'

'No, don't bother putting the telly off on my account. I've only come all the way round here to look at the backs of your heads.'

'See what I mean? He's been like this for weeks.'

'What's that on your neck, Gillian?'

'Gillian, your Grandma's talking to you.'

'What?'

'What's that horrible thing on your neck?'

'Nothing.'

'It's a disgrace. That's what it is. I told you people'd keep asking you about it. Letting some fairground gyppo do a thing like that to you.'

'What? A lad did it?'

'Gyppo lout.'

'How did he do it?'

'We won't go into that, Ma, if you don't mind. I've had a basinful. She's been sneaking off every time I've turned my back. And he's been no help. He's had his head stuck in his flipping books.'

'I can tell you how the gyppo did it, Grandma.'

'Thank you, Susan, but Grandma doesn't want to hear about it.'

'I do know though.'

'That's enough. We're not talking about that any more.'

'Digs all right?'

'Very nice. He wasn't happy though.'

'I don't know why you didn't do your usual. At least with a caravan you know the sheets are clean.'

'No, it was very nice. Spotless, really.'

'Grandad?'

'Yes, my duck.'

'I did great at swimming.'

'Did you? Nice warm water, was it?'

'Yeah.'

'No jellyfishes?'

'No.'

'How many miles can you swim now then?'

'Not *miles*, Grandad. I can do three widths.'

'How about you, young lady? Gillian? You been swimming?'

'Nah.'

'Well you should have done. Swimming's very good exercise. And the water might have washed that nasty mark off your neck.'

'Bog off.'

'What did you say to your Grandad?'

'Nothing?'

'I don't think it was nothing. Ron, did you hear what she said to your father?'

'I'm buggered if I can hear anything over this racket on the telly.'

'Gillian, apologize to your Grandad.'

'No, no. She's all right. I shouldn't have teased her.'

'I never said nothing.'

'I heard what she said.'

'Susan, be quiet. Gillian, apologize.'

'Sorry.'

'That's all right. Forget it. Only you should have gone swimming. It's a very fine thing to do. The new lady in the bungalow next door, she's got medals for her swimming from when she was your age.'

19

'She's had him round there, shifting settees. At his age.'

'Only being neighbourly. She's got medals for front crawl and butterfly. And life-saving.'

'Shifting settees and he ends up looking at swimming medals.'

'It was a settee, not settees. Just the one. You know?'

'Aren't you getting on with her then, Ma?'

'I'm not interested in getting on with her. There's no call.'

'You've not fallen out with her?'

'Not as such.'

'Do you like your letter rack?'

'Shifting settees. When did you ever know him do anything with a settee except fall asleep on it? He's only doing it to be contrary.'

'Well this is it. I mean, Ron's been the same. Nothing's been right for him this holiday. Whatever I've wanted to do, he's wanted to do something else. I begged him to come round the shops with me, but No, he hates shopping and he's got studying he wants to get on with, and then I get back to the beach, Susan's on her own and all red on her shoulders because he's not put any sun stuff on her, and he's round the back of the bucket and spade stall, helping some Gina unpack Mars Bars.'

Ronnie and Pop, guilty as charged, eyes front, feet tapping, minds a million miles away.

V ic Shires, ambling across the unsurfaced road of Plots 10 to 25 Crown Leys Council Estate, with a tea can in his hand and a smile on his face. Ronnie Glover, emptying his brush onto the back of a door and whistling through his teeth. Wednesday. Liver and onions, and *The Dick Van Dyke Show* with Mary Tyler Moore.

'Wrap them dancer's legs around me, Mary, and hold on tight.'

'Eh?'

He'd forgotten Pearce was there, painting the outside of the window frame.

'I was just telling Mary, liver and onions tonight.'

Pearce, leaning in, looking for Mary.

'How do you know it's liver and onions?'

'Because it's Wednesday, Pearce. Monday's cold joint. Tuesday's stew. Wednesday's liver. Thursday's sausage, Friday's chips.'

'What's Saturday?'

'Fry-up. Egg, bacon, beans, black pudding . . .'

'Kidney?'

21

'No, I hate kidney. No. Bacon, black pudding, did I say beans? Beans, egg and dippy.'

'Yeah, dippy! I love dippy.'

'Everybody loves dippy, Pearce. That's what kept us going in the war. The thought of coming home to dippy. What have you got tonight then?'

'Pasty.'

'Cornish?'

'Co-op. Diane gets them. The bashed ones.'

'She courting yet, your Diane?'

'What?'

'Has she got a bloke?'

'Don't think so.'

'Your Mum's never going to get rid of any of you lot, is she? How does she fit you all in?'

'Alan's on nights.'

'Yeah?'

'Diane's in with Mum and Shirley. I'm in with Grandad. And Gerald's in with Alan. He's on days and Alan's on nights.'

'So how do they go in when it's Alan's night off?'

'Don't know. Just squash up.'

'And how old's Shirley now?'

'About twenty-five or something.'

'Never. She must be thirty. Must be. I remember her in the Coronation pageant. Time you got shot of her.'

'How do you mean?'

'Find her a bloke. Fix her up. Her first, then Diane. Then you could move in to . . . no, your Mum'd have to move in with your Grandad, no, that's no good. Wouldn't help you really, would it? It's the old coffin-dodger you need to move out. He's the one. Then you'd have a bed to yourself. Any sign of Shires and that tea?'

'Yeah. He's just come back with it. Ron?'

'What?'

'Who's Mary?'

'What kept you?'

'Eh?'

'The tea, Victor. Get a shuffle on with that tea. I can see from your smile who you got to mash it for you.'

'Plot 14, bonny lad.'

'I know.'

'38D cup and big brown eyes.'

'I know.'

'She says, "Mr Painter" . . .' Vic Shires in a string vest and a falsetto voice. ' "Mr Painter," she says, "have you got a drop of white paint you can let me have for the kitchen cabinet?" I says, "I'll see what I can do for you, pet, and can I crave another small boon of you while that kettle's coming to the boil?" '

'Yeh?'

'I says, "Could I trouble you for a look at this week's *Titbits*?" and she says, "Help yourself." So there was this story in it, right? A man was driving home, deserted road, America somewhere, eating a hotdog, right? Engine dies on him, plenty of juice, but it just dies on him. Then, there's a bright light and he gets lifted up out of his motor by these creatures from outer space, like humans only with webbed feet and no nostrils, up into a flying saucer. They took him to some breeding station the other side of the universe, strapped him down, gave him some bright green drink, and then these hundreds of Martian women had it off with him, drained him dry, and when he came to he was back in his car and his hotdog was still warm.'

'Fancy.'

'It was Nebraska or somewhere.'

'She's a big girl, that Plot 14. I wouldn't mind her asking me for a drop of paint. You could have been well in there.'

'Not me, Ronald. Don't need it. My old lady is 38D cup all over.'

Eileen Glover, crying in her kitchen, in a pale blue short-sleeved jumper and a skirt off Leicester market. Susan Glover, reading out her school report for the third time.

'History, B plus. A very hardworking member of class. Maths, A minus. Another excellent term's work, Susan. English, A. An outstandingly able pupil. Science, B plus. Requires more confidence in practical work. Music, B minus. Making quick good progress on the piccolo.'

'That don't sound right. Let me look at that.' Gillian Glover, leafing through *Valentine* and scraping her legs with a Contessa Depilatory Mitt.

'What?'

'Quick good progress. That don't sound right. Let me have a look.'

'No. French, A minus. Consistently high standard. Geography, B . . .'

'Susan, set the table.'

'In a minute. Geography, B. Good accurate work.'

'Gillian, set the table. Your Dad'll be home.'

'See! Making *quite* good progress on the piccolo. That says quite good, not quick good. I've never heard you. What can you play?'

'B, A, G and D.'

'What?'

'B, A, G and D. The notes, dimmo.'

'But what can you play? You can't play nothing.'

'Double negative! Double negative!'

'What? What are you talking about? Here, look at this. Physical Education, D minus. Must try harder. You can't even get over a hurdle. I've seen you.'

'Could if I wanted to.'

'What a spaz.'

'Dad's home.'

Ronnie, wheeling his bike round the back, past the empty Tizer bottles lined up ready for the Fizzy Pop man (alternate Thursdays, late afternoon) and into the shed in spite of Gums, weaving and fawning and barking himself into a lather of love and excitement.

'All right. All right. Go steady or you'll leg me over.'

Inside, Susan is laying the table with a seersucker cloth, John Constable place mats, salt and pepper, and mustard, even though it's not Sunday, nor even Monday. Gillian is inspecting the damage to her legs. Eileen is still crying.

'Got my report, Dad. It's excellent.'

'Did you? Good girl. I shall only have to thrash you a couple of times tonight then. Eileen? Blarting again? What is it this time? Elvis still not written?'

'Onions.'

'Ooh, Eileen. I love it when you talk onions. Love it. And your nose goes all red when you're frying them. Did anybody ever tell you?'

'Susan's got her report.'

'She said. I'll look at it after. After I've had my tea and before

25

my assignation with Mary Tyler Moore, with her long silky legs and her big toothy smile. Are you jealous, Eileen? Are you?'

'Are you going to get washed or am I going to give this liver to the dog?'

'I'm going. Look. Here I go.'

'Good.'

'Eileen?'

'What?'

'Have we got dead thick gravy with burnt oniony bits in it?'

Ronnie and Eileen, side by side under a slippy-slidey counterpane that matches the curtains. Ronnie, hot, not really tired, tormented by visions of slender legs and elegant feet in little Italian shoes, and bottoms shaped like a pear, and warm lipsticky lips. Eileen, cold, in spite of the heatwave. Always cold. With purple feet and icicle fingers.

'How come your hands are so cold?'

'Bad circulation. Same as my Mum. That's why I get chilblains. My Mum used to cry with her chilblains in the winter.'

Mary's hands wouldn't be cold. Hers would be just the right sort of cool. Playful, but firm. Any time you like, Mary.

Ronnie Glover rolling nonchalantly into the folds of Eileen's nightie, pressing himself to the smooth, chilly lard of her bum.

'You can pack that in.'

'You know Fierce Pearce? He's only having to sleep with his Grandad. And his sisters are bunked up with his Mum. And then the other two, Alan and whassisname, they're doing musical beds, one on nights and one on days. The sheets must be warm all the time round their place. I reckon we'll finish Crown Leys next week. There's not a lot left to do.'

'Anyway, cold hands make the best pastry.'

'Night.'

'Night.'

26

Sunday. Roast chicken, peas and potatoes, roast and mash, Paxo stuffing, gravy, apple pie and custard and half an hour's shut-eye with Jimmy Clitheroe on the wireless.

Glebe Crescent, still resting from an afternoon at eighty in the shade, sealed up for the sabbath. Windows shut, against flies, wasps and the sound of ice-cream vans. Curtains drawn to stop the cushions fading. Minds closed, to be on the safe side. Only Ma out front, with a tin of ant powder in her hand.

'Are you winning?'

'I'd given you up.'

'I've brought your wallpaper. I thought I'd make a start.'

Ronnie, with five rolls of Anaglypta and a bag of runner beans.

'Not now you can't. Pop's watching telly.'

'What are you up to?'

'Ants.'

'Can't see any.'

'We're lousy with them. They've had all the alyssums, all the lobelias. I suppose you want a cup of tea?'

'What do they do? Do they eat them? Or drag them off somewhere? You never see them, do you? Funny that. So how come they've had all your stuff and hers next door is all right? Hers are a picture.'

'Jammy.'

'You should ask her. Ask her what her secret is.'

'She's just that jammy type. She's not from round here you know?'

'I know. You keep telling me.'

'They reckon she sold a great big house in Ashby de la Zouch and got herself this. Money in the bank and then got rehoused. Knows somebody on the council. Must do.'

'You keep telling me that too.'

'Stands to reason.'

'And that's it then, is it?'

'What?'

'If you're a rich widow from Ashby and you know somebody on the council, they won't bother you.'

'Who?'

'Ants.'

Through the kitchen. Newspaper on the floor. Precaution against dogs' doings. Into the sitting-room. Axaloom offcut to protect the carpet. Runner of clear plastic Hometect to save the Axaloom. Pop, watching the hymns, in an armchair with loose covers and polythene over the bits people lean on. The chair is protected from Pop and Pop is protected from the chair.

'Son.'

'I've brought the wallpaper.'

'The girls haven't been round.'

'Susan's coming. She's got her report. She'll be round.'

'Is the kettle on?' *Awake my soul, and with the sun, thy daily stage of duty run. Shake off dull sloth . . .*

'Don't bother for me, Ma. Nor for him. He's got a treble in that

28

glass he's forgotten about. You don't want tea. You've got Scotch. Graveney got his century then.'

'Mm.'

'You want to be careful with that ant powder though, Ma. You don't want to get it on your hands.'

'Bloody ant powder. There's not an insect left alive out there. It's not a question of ants. It's her face as makes everything shrivel up.'

'What, Ma? Or the Duchess next door?'

Pop laughing. His poor dry old lips gumming together at first, and his few strands of hair, greased back along his crown, making contact, just the slightest contact, with the plastic covering the back of his chair. Pop laughing and wheezing, the air going in easier than it comes out, eyes watering.

'She's all right. The Duchess. She enjoys a drink.'

'What are you watching this for?'

'I was just sat here and it come on. Better than sitting looking at that old scowler. Have you ever had Irish coffee, son?'

From the kitchen the sound of Ma making a pot of tea that Pop doesn't need and Ronnie doesn't want.

'Strong black coffee, nice and hot, with a good slug of Irish, sipped through a deep cold head of cream.'

'Oh yes? Where've you been reading about that?'

'Not reading about it, son. Sipping it. Me and the Duchess.'

'Get away.'

'It's the truth.'

'You and the Duchess?'

Lead kindly light, amid the encircling gloom, lead thou me on . . .

'You've never.'

'It's the truth.' *Keep thou my feet. I do not ask to see the distant scene. One step enough for me . . .*

'How'd you manage to slip your chain then?'

'Dressed the bolster in me jimmies and tippytoed out.'

'How much Scotch have you had?'

'What? Hardly any. Hardly worth wetting the glass. No, what

29

happened was, Ma was down the doctor's and the Duchess had a little job she needed doing. So after I'd been round her hinges with my can of Duckhams, she kindly invited me to partake of a nice hot brew. Irish coffee. Gaelic. Champion.'

Ma, with a tray, slopping weak tea into three saucers.

'Has he told you?'

'What? I said No to tea, Ma.'

'He's had another do. Didn't get to the toilet in time.'

'What did you need the doctor's for, Ma?'

'Cotton wool.'

'What for?'

'I like to have some in. No sense in paying for it. We're entitled. We've paid in. I should have told him about Pop. Asked him for a rubber sheet. I shall do next time.'

'He doesn't need anything like that.'

'He will do. He sits in front of that telly and he gets that engrossed he leaves it too late. I have to remind him. You're not here. You don't know. If I didn't remind him he'd never go.'

Pop, looking smaller suddenly and tired. Not like a man who'd recently oiled a duchess's hinges. Ignoring his cup of tea. Watching the credits of *Praise Be*. Muttering into his glass.

'Ah shut up, you prune-faced old bag. I only do it to annoy you. And I like the feel of it. Pissing your pants. Lovely.'

'What did he say?'

'I don't know.'

'Pissing your pants, pissing your pants, pissing, pissing, pissing your pants. Telling me to go to the lav every five minutes. Guildford cathedral! Guildford bloody cathedral! It was a repeat. A bloody buggering repeat.'

'See what I mean?'

Ronnie, cycling home from Ma and Pop's for tinned pears and Carnation and *The Arthur Haynes Show* with Joe 'Mr Piano' Henderson.

Something's got into Pop. Trouble. Age. Might be. How old is he? 1893. Add seven for the century. 1962. Add sixty-two. Seven add sixty-two is sixty-nine. That's not old. Or is 1893 Ma? Ma's older. He does dribble in his trousers sometimes. Lazy, Eileen says. Wrapped up in the telly and then he's left it too late. But all that cheek to Ma. That's not like Pop. He always said he knew which side his bread was buttered. Yes Ma. Just coming Ma. Are you all right there Ma? Always Ma first. Ma and Pop. Ma and Pop, Pegwell Bay, August 1919. Ma and the girls in the machine room, Thornton's, 1922. Ma with Gran. Ma with Uncle Albert. Ma with Gillian and Susan. And always Ma. Never Dorothy. Dot. Dolly. He couldn't have called her Ma before they were married. He says he did. Like she was his *Ma. Like she looked after him. But she never did. Only one person Ma ever looked after.*

'Where's your Mam?'

'*In the Snug.*'

'*What are you doing?*'

'*Waiting here. Ma said to.*'

'*Come down Akeman Street. Ratcliffe's found a dead cat.*'

'*No. I've got to stop here.*'

Parked on the step of the Earl of Granby with a bottle of Vimto and a threat.

'*Sit still. Don't play in the gutter. Don't wander off, getting into trouble. Make that Vimto last you.*'

And then the release.

'*Go home now and get to bed. Go on. I shan't be long. Straight home. If you don't, the Ten O'Clock Horses'll get you.*'

'*Don't let them get me, Ma. I sat still. I'll go straight home. Don't say you can hear the horses coming. Don't, Ma. I've been good. Where's my Pop? Will Pop come home too? I like it when Pop tells me about the olden days.*'

'*I'll tell you about the olden days, boy. I was the fastest machinist Thornton's had ever had and I didn't plan on falling for you. I used to tell him to pull it out quick, and I used to move myself out of the way, because he was that slow and stupid, your Pop. But I still got caught.*'

'*Don't tell the next bit, Ma.*'

'*When I knew I'd fallen for you, I drank this town dry of gin, and I jumped off chairs and down the stairs, but you'd got your claws well and truly dug in. There was no shaking you. But you never made no difference to me. I wore a corset all the way through, and the week before I had you a coalman stopped me on West Bridge and offered me a bag of slack if he could give me a poke. Oh yes. I kept my figure.*'

'*You did, Ma. But don't tell about when I was born. Just tell about Aunty Pearl.*'

'*When you were born, you ripped me all inside. The nurse had never seen anything like it, and she had to send for Doctor Swift, so that was more expense. He said I was lucky you hadn't killed me, and I should never ever have another one. So that put a stop* to all that pushing and shoving of a Friday night. And then they bound me tight, up above and down below, and I sent you round to Aunty Pearl. I was back at Thornton's before you were three weeks old.'

'And Aunty Pearl fed me, Ma, and snuggled me up and rocked me. I played with clothes-pegs on her kitchen floor and she used to make bunny rabbit blancmanges with currant eyes for me and the other boys and girls, and she sang songs to us and played them on her old piano. I loved my Aunty Pearl.

'Aunty Pearl ruined you. Made you soft. She'd never give you a tap. Didn't matter what you did. I was paying her and I still had to straighten you out.'

'Yeah. Tell it all, Ma. Tell how you took Pop's razor strop to me, and how you fell out with Aunty Pearl and everybody else. Tell how you always fell out with people and nobody liked you, and you always sent me when you wanted stuff on tick. Tell how I had to have my shirts from the woman who bought dead men's clothes and have them cut down. Tell how I always made my Vimto last and then ran home fast as I could because the Ten O'Clock Horses were after me. But they never got me. They never, never got me. Tell it, Ma. Look. I'm not crying. I'm not. I'm not.'

Ronnie Glover, cycling past the big new bungalow on Gartree Road, with dry eyes and a tight, heavy ache in the middle of his chest, not noticing the board on its gate that says THE PONDEROSA NO HAWKERS. Not noticing that the woman chivvying two miniature poodles across the front lawn has the long, slender legs of a dancer.

33

V ic and Ronnie and Fierce Pearce scoffing corned beef sandwiches and melted Penguins over a can of strong stewed tea.

'How did you go on yesterday?'

'Won by seven runs.'

'Yeh?'

'Took two catches.'

'Yeh? How many did you make?'

'One of their openers looped his second ball and I took it at gully, sweet as a nut. Then their number 6. Little goatee beard and ran like he'd shat himself. I dropped him once and then I had him, next over. He hooked it high to square leg and I had him.'

'And how many did you make?'

'A few.'

Vic Shires, Mr Not Out, No Runs of the Dog & Gun Sunday XI. A phlegmatic tail-ender, nippy in the field, with a notable bowling action and a wife who does excellent teas.

'You should come along one of these Sundays.'

'Yeh?'

'Bring Eileen and the girls.'

'Eileen wouldn't wear that.'

' 'Course she would. She'd love it. Bring a deck-chair and her knitting. She'd love it.'

'I did used to play a bit. When I came out of the Navy. I used to bowl a bit.'

'We've got plenty of bowlers. But if you was to come along a few Sundays. Play yourself in. And then if somebody didn't turn up . . . I couldn't make any promises but, you know, come along, see how you go.'

'Yeah, well, maybe.'

'We've had people queueing up to play for us. It's a good little side. But I could put a word in. Get you a try.'

'I wouldn't mind a game, Vic.'

Fierce Pearce, bright and eager, with more than a passing look of a young Ken Barrington.

'You come along on Sunday then, lad.'

'I will. Are you coming, Ronnie? We could both go.'

'I don't know. I'm paperhanging round Ma's. And we might have something on. You know. I'd have to check with Eileen.'

Ronnie Glover, worrying whether life will be long enough to learn Italian and do good drawings and play cricket for the Dog & Gun. Ronnie, practising his off-drive with a length of dowelling and wondering whether Plot 14 would like another little drop of paint.

'So can I?'

'It's up to your Dad.'

'But he'll say it's up to you.'

'It's a lot of money, Susan. That's the thing.'

'It's three shillings. Three shillings for ballet and three shillings for tap, but if you do both you get it for five shillings.'

'What I'm saying is, it won't stop at three shillings. You'd have to have the shoes. And then there'd be the other stuff. The little skirts and that.'

'The shoes aren't much. They're about ten shillings.'

'Susan . . .'

'Or they're about two pounds. You can have pink or red, but you're not allowed white until you go on blocks and that's not for ages and ages because if you do you can wreck your toes and be a cripple afterwards. They're putting a show on after the summer. With proper make-up and everything. Go on, Mum.'

'That's what I mean. It'd be nothing but spend.'

'It won't. It won't. I promise.'

'And then Gillian'll want the same. There's just not the money for it, Susan.'

'Gillian won't.'

'I won't what?'

Gillian Glover, aged fifteen, wearing a Valderma face-pack and a quilted housecoat, looking for something to spoil her tea.

'Ballet and tap.'

'What for?'

'To learn them. To be in shows and that.'

'Where?'

'The Jacqueline Granger School of Dance.'

'When?'

'Wednesdays and Saturdays.'

'Naah. Too much on. What do you want to do it for anyway? You can't dance.'

'That's what I want to go for, stupid. That is usually why you go to a school. To learn it.'

'You're the one who's stupid. You'd be rubbish. Anyway, where you going to do that crap. You going to go out with some boy and do ballet dancing. Eh? Go out with a boy and do *Swan Lake*? That's rubbish dancing, that is. Where'd you get that jumper? That's mine, you cow.'

'I'm only trying it.'

'Take it off, you little slapper.'

'I'm only having a lend of it.'

'Take it off. And the ring. And the scent.'

'God, Gillian. You are so thick. So can I, Mum? She doesn't want to, so there'd only be me. And if Grandy gives me some money for a good report I can put it towards the shoes. Can I?'

'I'm going to bloody kill her. She's got my jumper. She's been round all my stuff. And she's done the quiz in *Valentine*.'

'Never.'

'You bloody did.'

'Gillian!'

37

'I can see where you've rubbed your answers out. And you're a liar. You even lie when you do other people's quizzes.'

'Do not.'

'You're a liar and a thief and I bloody hate you. You're not allowed in my room ever again. Did you hear that, Mum? She's banned. And if she goes in there again I'll break her bloody neck.'

'What about the classes, Mum? Shall we tell Dad?'

'Tell her, Mum. She's banned.'

'Will you both shut up? Give it a rest. How can I concentrate on this with the pair of you fighting and carrying on?'

Eileen Glover, with a harassed frown and a pleated skirt, standing in her kitchen ironing tea towels.

'Eileen, I'm putting this here to dry. Right? I don't want it where it'll get dog hairs on it.'

'What is it?'

'Hardboard. I've just undercoated it.'

'What's it for?'

'A painting.'

'You can't paint.'

'What do you mean. I'm a skilled craftsman.'

'Yes, but that's *that* sort of painting. You can't paint pictures. Can you?'

'Never know till you try, do you?'

'What will it be of?'

'Haven't decided.'

'You're supposed to start with a bowl of fruit.'

'Are you? Who says?'

'Everybody.'

'We haven't got a bowl of fruit.'

'No. Susan wants dancing lessons. It's three shillings a week if she just does ballet, five shillings if she does tap as well.'

'I could paint Gums. If he'd sit still.'

'I don't want a picture of him. He's under my feet all day. I don't need a painting anyway. So what do you think?'

'What?'

'The dancing lessons.'

'She could do. No harm. Can we manage it, do you reckon?'

'It might be a five-minute wonder. She could have a go. As long as we don't have to spend out too much.'

'Where is it?'

'The Jacqueline Granger School of Dance. Over the Co-op. It used to be Billiards.'

'Did it?'

'You know. They've had scaffolding all over it.'

'Do I? What about Gillian?'

'She's not interested.'

'I could do a self-portrait.'

'You will not. If I've got to have a painting in my lounge I want something nice. Can't you do me a nice view. You could do some trees and some little lambs and baby horses. Can you do horses?'

'Don't think so.'

'I like views.'

'Trouble is, Eileen, I haven't got any views in my life, have I? Not lambs and trees, anyhow. The back of our shed. That's the view I've got. And artists have to be true to themselves. We have to paint the Gums and garden sheds we truly know. See?'

'Well I like views.'

'And I like bums. Nice tight ones that jut out. And big ones that hang lower. Proper bums. I'll paint a woman with a proper bum.'

'Ron!'

'A great big fat bare bum.'

'Not in my lounge you won't.'

'You might like it. You might want to show it to the neighbours. You never know. Anyway, how about it?'

'What?'

'You know.'

'What?'

'It's Friday night.'

'Is that all you ever think about?'

'It is on Friday nights.'

'Well if you're quick. I've been ironing all afternoon.'

'I can be.'

'And quiet.'

'Yes.'

'No shouting.'

'No.'

'And no saying those words.'

'No.'

'Fetch a towel then. Not a good one.'

Ronnie and Eileen Glover, locked in silent copulation on a length of old roller towel.

'Have you finished yet? Ron? Is it you making that noise?'

Gums Glover, aged seven and a half, engaged in noisy personal hygiene four inches from the edge of the roller towel, awaiting his master's voice.

'Yesss!'

Blackberries, acorns and blowsy roses, drawn in sepia and tightly packed on a background of cream.

'How about this then? Eh?'

'It's a bit busy. It's all right. But we've got the Anaglypta.'

'You can still have your Anaglypta. I've only got two rolls of this. So you can have one wall of this and three in Anaglypta. Eh? It was in the oddments box at Walters'. Look at the quality of it. This'll hang like fabric.'

'I don't know. I've never heard of one wall odd. They'll think we run out of paper.'

'No they won't. It's the fashion now. I've seen it in a luxury ocean-view apartment on *Hawaiian Eye*. It's called Contemporary.'

'It looks dear. I'm not having it if it's dear.'

'It's not anything. Not to you. You know that. Should we ask Pop though? See if he's agreeable?'

'Save your breath. He don't know about wallpaper.'

'Where is he?'

'Having a lie-down.'

'Is he not well?'

'I don't know. He's either having a lie-down or he's dropped off in front of the telly, dribbling in his trousers. He's never opened his library book. And then he's up and down all night making pots of tea. He's getting to be a very aggravating man. You don't know. You're never here.'

'I'm here now.'

'Eileen never comes round.'

'Eileen's very busy, Ma. She's supervising school dinners.'

'That's not all day. That's a pin-money job. I used to do eight till six at Thornton's. I brought more home than he did.'

'Yeh, but. She's got a lot on. You know. The girls and everything. She'll be round.'

'Nobody knows what I have to put up with. You get old and nobody bothers with you. You'll find out. I wish I was back at Thornton's. I had twenty girls under me. Twenty.'

'Do you want this wallpaper or what?'

'It won't cost us extra?'

'Nothing of it's costing you anything.'

'Go on then.'

'Right. I'm going to get this lot stripped off and then I'll come by tomorrow night and slap a bit of size on. So you get off now. Go and get some fresh air. I'll wake Pop. I'll make a start and then I'll take him a cup of tea.'

'I'll just cover my chairs.'

'*I'll* cover the chairs. You get off. Go and have a sit in the Gardens. There was a silver band setting up when I come by. Go on. I want to make a start.'

Ma Glover, moving a gift from Cleethorpes to a place of safety. Refolding the *News of the World*. Straightening dust covers.

'I'm just wondering whether to rinse a few stockings through before I go.'

'Ma!'

Ronnie, moving furniture, making up sugar soap, laying out brushes and scrapers, confident and expert, absorbed in the thoroughness of his preparations, whistling 'In a Monastery Garden'.

'Son?'

The bedroom door, open a crack.

'Thought you were asleep.'

'Has she gone?'

'Yeah. Do you want a brew?'

'No, no. How long's she been gone?'

'Just. Put the kettle on. I could murder one.'

'Say where she was going?'

'How are you doing?'

'Champion. Say how long she'd be?'

'She's gone for a sit in the Gardens. There's a band playing.'

'You're getting on well there, son. Do you want a hand?'

'No, you're all right. Just make a brew. Do you want to have a look at the wallpaper?'

'What for? It's that bobbly stuff again. Isn't it that bobbly stuff we've got in the bedroom?'

'Yeah. But there's another sort as well, just for the one wall.'

'Is there?'

'On the side. In the kitchen. Have a decko.'

'Mm. Very nice.'

'No, unroll it a bit more. See? What do you think?'

'That's all right, is it? One wall different?'

'It's called Contemporary.'

'Is it?'

'How's your waterworks?'

'Lovely. How's yours?'

'You know what I mean. Ma's worried about you. You know. And she says you're sleeping all day and banging about all night.'

'Bollocks. Have they declared?'

'They hadn't. They were four hundred and something for four. Cowdrey done well.'

'They'll declare. It's in the bag. Four hundred and fifty. That'll do. Trounced them.'

'So you're happy with that other paper then?'

'Yes. Suits me. Contemporary. There we are, son. I'll leave it there for you. Leave it to brew a bit. I've just got to nip out.'

Pop, stopped in his tracks by the kitchen door swinging open after the briefest of knocks.

'It's only me.'

The Duchess of Ashby de la Zouch, in a nylon blouse and a sweetheart pinny.

'Did you remember about that tap, Archie? I hate to be a nuisance but it's getting harder and harder to turn it off and I'm wondering if it's even going to last till the council offices open. Hello.'

'This is my big son.'

'I know. I've seen him in and out.'

'I was just on my way round, wasn't I, son?'

'Well I do hate to trouble you, especially on a weekend, but I can't do washers. I always say you need a big strong man for washers. Mrs G all right? It must be very nice having a son who can call in and look after you. My daughter's in Canada, but there we are. And you're in the middle of decorating. Is this what you're having? Very eye-catching. I've got a beautiful paper in my lounge, haven't I, Archie? Eighteen shillings a roll, but worth every penny. You must come and see it some time.'

'He's got to get on. Got to get cracking. Haven't you, son?'

Archie Glover, risen like a phoenix from the ashes of Pop, taller, straighter, pinker, and suddenly capable of conveying to his son, with silent authority, that this would not be a good time to go viewing eighteen-bob wallpaper.

'So I'll just be next door having a look at Beryl's tap. I'll change her washer and be back directly. Don't let that tea go cold.'

* * *

Beryl? Archie? *Changing washers?*

Ronnie, alone in his mother's kitchen, annoyed, excited, and too hot in his overalls, pouring himself a cup from a nice pot of freshly boiled water, prepared by a man whose mind had drifted away from the tea caddy to plumper nylon-clad things.

*B*reakfast is la prima colazione *or simply* la colazione. *However,* colazione *is sometimes used for the midday meal, traditionally the main meal of the day. More commonly though the lunchtime meal is called* il pranzo. *Similarly, a substantial evening meal may be called* il pranzo, *but if, typically, it is lighter,* la cena *is generally used.* Il pranzo *normally consists of four courses;* il primo piatto – *usually soup, or a pasta dish;* il secondo piatto – *usually meat or fish;* il contorno – *vegetables, or a salad; and* il dolce, *the dessert – usually fresh fruit, except in restaurants and on special occasions at home.*

'Whatever is up with you?'

'Nothing.'

'Don't you want that pork pie?'

'No.'

'I'll have it.'

'Where's Susan?'

'Round Annette's.'

'Where's Gillian?'

'Out. You had a run-in with Ma?'

'No.'

'Papering going all right?'

'Yes.'

'I'll have that piece of pork pie if you like.'

'Yes.'

Ronnie, robbed of his appetite, unable to tell Eileen why he has a dull, hot headache, because he doesn't know himself.

'Does she like the paper?'

'Yeh. She doesn't mind.'

'Did she say how Pop was?'

'Same as usual.'

'Ron?'

'What?'

'Buck up. It's not like you to leave spring onions.'

'I'm going down to the shed for a bit.'

'I'll save your Battenberg for later on. I think you've caught a little chill. Susan, you're late for your tea.'

Susan, hungry and full of important news, taking bread and butter before she sits down. 'Annette's got her tap shoes and I had a go in them. They're brilliant. And you have to have the shoes before you can start the classes because Madame says, so we'll have to get them before Saturday. Is there any pickle?'

'But I've already told you, Susan, we're not buying fancy shoes till we know if you're going to stick at it. That ping-pong set was a five-minute wonder. You can wear your pumps for a few weeks. And you can have your Dad's onions. He's caught a chill.'

'I have to have the shoes. I have to.'

'Ron, will you speak to her about this?'

But Ron is already on his way to the shed, to be in a place where Frank Ifield won't be singing 'I Remember You'. A place where he can hold his head and think about things and not have to peel the marzipan off his Battenberg cake and then eat it, yellow square, pink square, yellow square, pink.

A fresh piece of paper, cool and smooth, inviting him to do his best drawing ever. A nice sharp pencil.

The pencil is a linear tool and by its response to pressure will make a variety of lines. Holding the pencil close to its lead, resting your hand on the paper, is the correct way for detailed drawing. By holding the pencil nearer its blunt end you are freer to draw from the elbow or the shoulder and make more sweeping lines.

The smell of damp magazines and Robbo's bonfire. The sound of the Lyons Maid ice-cream van.

'Please don't let anyone come and ask me if I want a vanilla cornet.'

Choose a standing pose to begin with. This makes it easier to see how the weight is carried. Look for the essential elements of the pose, such as the swing of the back and hips. Draw these with simple strokes.

Mary Tyler Moore. What would it be like to know a woman like that, standing there in her swishy skirts, calling you Honey, all ready to fix you a drink? What would it be like to have one of those settees you could stretch out on, full length, and a woman you could nuzzle on that little place where the back of her neck dips in, and a drinks' tray on the side? How would it be, living without a pouffe and last Christmas's nuts still sitting on the sideboard like some prize fucking exhibit and a Ma who's never had a good word to say about anything in her whole life, only you've got to keep humouring her because you're just about all she's got in the world?

Note that the feet are normally set obliquely to the leg, rather than pointing directly forward, and the ankle bone is higher on the inside of the foot than the outside.

'Fuck it. Fuck it, fuck it, fuck it.'

Ronnie, getting the ankles wrong again, screwing up the paper so hard his knuckles turn white, stamping his feet, wiping the tears on his arm, and then stopping still, listening to the terrible urgent sniffling and snuffling of love trying to get under the door. Gums, who hasn't had a kind word all day, needing to make things better, yipping and chewing on the rotten wood, until Ronnie gets slowly to his feet and lets him in.

'It's all shit, Gums. Drawing's shit. Work's shit. Tea was shit. Even the old whassisname's shit. Do you fancy a bit of choccy?'

Gums, ears pricked, more at the general impression that the darkest hour is over, than at any particular word.

'Come on then. We'll go and see if Gibson's is still open. Get a bit of Fruit & Nut. Only don't tell Eileen.'

A man and his dog, slipping out the back way, down the jitty that runs past all the gardens. A quiet place, with overgrown privet and broken fences, with the light just dropping and midges in the air. Gums, careering ahead, then stopping and looking back to say, 'Hurry along now. Follow me. Where is it we're going?' And Ronnie, feeling a little bit better, but not a lot, whistling and planning to chuck out the Christmas nuts, and then noticing a couple, hard at it against the back of Murgatroyd's shed, clothed, but untucked and oblivious. Some boy in jeans. And a girl in a yellow spotted circular skirt. That was when he knew what had made his head throb. That was when he knew the thing that had made him be narky with Eileen and leave his pork pie, was the sight of Pop, on his way out of Ma's kitchen, in unseemly haste to take up tap-washer maintenance, with one hand – and of this there could be no doubt – with one hand cradling the Duchess's behind.

Susan Glover, with her dress tucked in her knickers, trying to do handstands against the wall of the garden shed, watched by three pairs of eyes. Gillian, sitting on the dustbin, bored, cracking bubble gum against her lips. Gums, hopeful but baffled, trying to work out his role in the handstand game. And Robbo, two gardens away, in his carpet slippers, pretending to disbud his chrysanthemums.

'I'll help you if you like.'

'What do you mean?'

'If you like I'll catch your legs.'

'No, it's all right.'

'I could get you doing it properly. Like this. Look.'

Gillian Glover, upside-down in a yellow spotted circular skirt and a pair of nylon knickers, 36-22-36, whichever way you looked at it.

'Get down quick, Gillian. Mr Robinson can see your bottom.'

'Can't hear you.'

'Get down. Get down. You're not supposed to stay upside-down that long. All the blood goes into your brain and makes it burst. Gillian.'

Gillian, returning to earth with languorous confidence, left leg, right leg, indifferent to her sister's panic, in no hurry to adjust her skirt or release Robbo Robinson from her long cool stare.

'Now you. I'll catch your legs.'

'No. I'm fed up with handstands.'

'Go on. I'll catch you. What's up? Are you frit?'

'No. I might do some tomorrow. Get's boring if you do too many.'

'Yeh. Handstands are dead boring. What are you going to do now?'

'Dunno.'

'Got any money?'

'No.'

'Want to look for some empties? Take 'em back to the Off?'

'Where?'

'In the shed?'

'How much would we get?'

'Depends.'

'Go halves?'

'Yeh. But I get the biggest half because I thought of it.'

'Are we allowed?'

'Jesus. What a dump.'

Gillian, Susan and Gums, on the threshold of the dark and private world of Ronnie Glover.

Cans; creosote, three; wood primer, four; undercoat, gloss and eggshell finish, nineteen assorted. Nails, screws, bolts, nuts, hinges, rawlplugs, washers, and handy little pieces of wood. Glass cutters, Allen keys, chisels, awls and pliers. Rope.

'We could skip.'

'Piss off.'

Fishing rods, chicken-wire, fire-irons (two sets), cider-press, Pogo stick, mandoline with one string.

'Here's a bottle.'

'There's something in it.'

'Might be gin.'

'No, look. It says lime juice. Only that's not lime juice. Lime juice is green.'

'Don't have to be. Have a taste.'

'No. That's dangerous. You must never taste things if you don't know what they are.'

'Go on. You'll be all right. Here. I'll pour a bit into this lid and get the dog to taste it. Here. Here you stupid bastard hound. Here.'

Gums Glover, out of there.

A watering can, half a rake, two fish tanks, a Pakamac, a pile of old *Picture Posts*, and a copy of *Life Drawing Simplified*.

'Here. Look at this.'

'Whose is it?'

'I bet Mum don't know he's got this. It's got everything in it.'

'Don't go so fast.'

'I'll turn the pages. I'll turn them. I'm the oldest. Aargh. God. That's disgusting.'

'Hold it still. Aargh!'

'Fancy having your drawing in a book when you've got a bum the size of that on you.'

'Are there any willies?'

'Hold on. Hold on. We're getting there. All right. Are you ready?'

'Show me.'

'Are you sure you're ready?'

'Gillian. Stop mucking about.'

'Ta-da!'

'Don't wobble it about. Yeah. Are there any more?'

'Have you ever seen one before?'

'No. Have you?'

'Loads. Here you are.'

'Whose?'

'What?'

'Whose have you seen?'

'I'm not telling you. How about this one? Is it like you thought it'd be?'

'Yeah.'

'Didn't you think it'd be bigger? Like a hosepipe?'

'Yeah.'

' 'Course, this is only a drawing. Photos are better. Look. Magazines. There might be some in here.'

'I don't think we're going to find any empties, do you, Gillian?'

Susan Glover, wondering whether she might find an old tennis ball. Gillian Glover, wondering whether she might find a photograph of a willy or a dead body or something good. Gums, stretched out in the sunshine, just wondering. No-one at all noticing a small, spiral-bound sketch pad containing some experimental pencil strokes, and Ronnie Glover's first nervy attempt at *Mary Tyler Moore, With Skirts Raised*.

'And once you've done it, you wonder how you ever managed before. Course, we had to start afresh with carpet, because the front room was mottledy grey and the living-room was green swirls, and we couldn't have them shouting at one another. Next door had the grey one off of us for their Kenneth because he's been off work for months with his nerves. There was hardly a mark on it. So now we're red, all the way through. Don't half make a difference. Any road, Jean says to me, "You know what this needs now, don't you? A bar. Our own bar, across the corner of the lounge." So that's next on the agenda. But what I'm actually thinking of doing is building a combined Drinks and Hi-Fi cabinet, so it all closes nice and neat, and everything's there when you need it, of an evening. Glasses. Mixers. Records. Cocktail cherries. Everything you need for a nice night in. See?'

Vic Shires, seated on a distemper can outside Plot 103, the Rowans, eating egg sandwiches that could have done with a bit of salt.

'Mm.'

'What do you reckon?'

'Mm.'

'Because all that stuff takes some storing. Bottles, and the little mats and all that. And we've got quite a collection of records. Alma Cogan. Pat Boone. Songs from the Shows. Legend of the Glass Mountain. And loads of Latin American. Stanley Black and his Orchestra. Xavier Cugat. Name any Latin American and we've got it. Edmundo Ros.'

'You really like that, do you?'

'Latin American?'

'Stopping in. Listening to records. You and Jean.'

'Yeah. Love it. Why? Don't you?'

'Nothing to play them on.'

'Well you want to get yourself something. You want to go in for stereophonic. It's the coming thing.'

'Gillian's got a little whassit. Dansette.'

'No. Gotta be stereophonic. Come with me into the world of Full Frequency Stereophonic Sound. There's this record you can get, with a train on it. Sounds like it's going straight across your lounge, right across in front of you. That's the stereo. You and Eileen want to treat yourselves, bonny lad.'

'No bloody money, bonny lad.'

'No? You're doing all right, aren't you? Working a few week-enders? Getting a bit extra?'

'I've got two girls, don't forget. Wanting baths every five minutes, and shoes and grub. Leaving lights on. It's different when you've got kids, Vic.'

'I suppose it is.'

'I wouldn't be without them. Don't get me wrong.'

'No. No.'

'But you're paying out all the time. It never lets up. And then, you know, they're always around. In and out. Well Susan is. You'd never get a quiet night in at our house. You and Jean never want kids?'

'No. Well. She had a bit of trouble, so it never cropped up. I

55

wouldn't have minded. Might have been nice really. But it never cropped up and it's not bothered us. We're golden, me and Jean. Twenty-two carat.'

'Me and Eileen are all right.'

' 'Course you are.'

'I mean, it's not everything, is it? The old whassisname.'

'Hello, Norrie. All set for Sunday?'

Fierce Pearce, flushed with importance, suddenly on first-name terms with Chater, the plasterer.

'Oh it's *Hello Norrie*, is it? How come?'

'Cricket.'

'Oh. Right.'

'He's our number 3 batsman.'

'Right. I thought it was Bernie Chater played for your lot, Vic?'

'We've got three of them. Chater N., Chater B., and Chater B. Senior.'

'Norrie bats number 3.'

'I believe you mentioned it, Pearce.'

'I had a lend of his pads and everything, didn't I, Vic?'

'Did you? Not his box?'

'What?'

'You didn't have a lend of his box?'

'Yeah. What? What?'

'Aarh, Pearce, you never. You don't want your old feller curled up inside Chater's abdominal protector. He's a plasterer. They're the scum of the earth, plasterers.'

'Norrie's all right.'

'Oh well. *Norrie* it is then. Just you mind you give it a good wipe-out before you tuck it down your kecks another time.'

'He's got a false bottom in his kit bag.'

'Has he?'

'Guess what he's got in there.'

'Doctored balls. Nose pickings.'

'Naah. Go on. Guess.'

'*Playboy?* The *Watchtower?*'

'Naah. D'you give up?'
'Yeh. Go on then.'
'Crunchie bars.'
'Never!'
'I seen them.'
'Eyes left, lads. Get a look at that.'

The toss of a head. A blouse undone a button too far. A girl
pushing a pram, taking the shortcut to The Sycamores, little pink
skirt, tail twitching, heels rapping on the concrete. Good skin on
her arms too. Pale and even. Leaning into the pram handle, against
the slope of Rowan Ride, hurrying home, uninterested in three
house painters on their break. Vic Shires, drawing a sketch of his
proposed Drinks and Hi-Fi cabinet in the margin of the *Daily
Mirror*. Ronnie Glover nursing a mug of hot tea and a stiffy the
size of Blackpool Tower. And Fierce Pearce, breathing through
his mouth, bathed in the glory of first-hand acquaintance with the
private confectionery preferences of Chater, N.

'What are we going to do tonight?'

'How do you mean?'

'Saturday night. We ought to do something. Vic and his old lady, they have a drink and listen to Pat Boone.'

'We haven't got any Pat Boone.'

'No. That was just a frinstance.'

'Well what then?'

'Anything. Go for a walk. Drop in somewhere for a drink. The Queen Adelaide.'

'We couldn't take Susan in there. We'd have to go somewhere with a garden.'

'There's always bloody something. I don't want to sit in a pub garden. I want to sit inside with the grown-ups, and I want you to have a proper drink, not just a Britvic. Anybody else can go out for a drink. It's not like flying to Acafuckingpulco, is it?'

'Oh well. If you're going to be like that.'

Eileen Glover, changing her cardigan and hardening her heart.

*H*air's going. Just a bit. Not so's you'd really notice. Only *Eileen. Said it was going identical to Pop's. On top, down the middle. Cheers, Eileen. It might not though, because it's not like Pop's. His is thin and gingery. Mine's dark and curly. And thick. Still quite thick. Chin's going. Belly's going. Thirty-seven. Still young. Fifteen-year-old daughter. Fifteen.* That's *young. Thirty-seven's nearly forty. Too late. Thirty-seven's nothing. Other blokes don't get like this. They get up, go to work, come home, have their tea, go to the pub. Two weeks in a caravan at Weymouth. They're contented. They never think about it. They've just got that all right thing inside of them, so they never think about it. All that stuff they're missing but they don't even know about it, so they're all right. I'm not. I'm bloody not. It might get easier. This might be the worst of it because thirty-seven's old and yet it's not. Forty-seven'll be easier. So you can just let things go and they won't eat at your guts any more. But thirty-seven. Too late to have a nice house and know how to drive a car and do good drawings and speak Italian and have some really good whassisname. That's all* *this is about. Admit it. No. Admit it. It's not. You don't give a monkey's about getting a leather settee and knowing about Art. You just want to dip your wick. I do. But it's not just that. It's really really not. It'd help though. Could learn to drive. Could do. Can't afford a motor. No. But you will afford one, in a few years' time. Then we could go for runs out. Me and Eileen. We're all right. A lot of men'd be glad to have Eileen. I'm glad. Yeah. She's a very kind person and she works very hard for all of us. Everything's clean and nice. She'd do anything for you, Eileen. Cook you a special. Clean up. Mend stuff. Anything. Except hold your balls when they feel like they're filling with concrete. I only want something nice. Something that turns out like it is on the telly. Like getting invites to parties where there's waiters and a swimming pool and women in tight frocks that you don't even know come up and dance with you. Or going for a drive just before dark and stopping to watch the sky turn green and the sea turn purple. Something. Just not pissing your life away with a nice clean woman who's never heard of Chianti. Pissing Saturday afternoon away, waiting for a thirteen-year-old because she can't walk home on her own because of murderers and that, hanging about when you could be going round an art gallery. What art gallery? What bloody art gallery? There's the museum. They've got paintings in there. Did have before the war. I could be having a mooch round there. You wouldn't be though. If Eileen could have fetched Susan, if she hadn't got to see to that cupboard because* somebody's *been mixing pillowcases up with tea towels, you wouldn't be going round any museum. You'd be watching* Grandstand *with the sound off. Hair's not bad from the front. Not bad at all.*

Ronnie, checking his reflection in Lipton's window, resolving to get a provisional driving licence, a bottle of bay rum, and a box of Newberry Fruits for Eileen, diving into a doorway and bounding up two flights of stairs.

'Let's have one last go at "Button Up Your Overcoat". Pay attention. And remember the back line start changing places on *Bootleg Hooch*. Hm? When you're ready, Mrs Stockwell. Toe heel ball change, toe heel ball change, Annette. Watch your hands. No doggy paws. Back line through to the front. Yes! And hold the line. Keep it tidy. Heads up. Smile. And . . . All right, girls. That was much better. Time to finish though. Girls. Don't twitter. Let's finish with our nice curtsey. If you please, Mrs Stockwell. And . . . Thank you. Good afternoon, class.'

'Good afternoon, Madame.'

'Now practise hard, but if you don't have a practice board be very very careful of Mummy's floor. And learn the words. I shall expect everyone to know them by next week. Don't leave anything behind. Linda, Jennifer Humphreys and the new Susan, see me now please.'

Ronnie, forced against the wall by a wave of gobby twelve-year-olds with shapeless faces and pointy little bosoms. All making their own way home. No Dads waiting. Not even any Mums. Nobody else hanging about feeling like a spare prick at a wedding and missing the classified results.

'Is this your Daddy, Susan?'

Jacqueline Granger, tall and dark, with a waist and a neck, and little lines round her eyes, and a great wide red smiley mouth crowded with big strong teeth.

'I'm glad I caught you. Shoes, Daddy. I'm afraid we can't take her without the proper shoes. Barratts have got them. Or Freeman Hardy. Tell Mummy she'll be able to get them at most shoe shops in town. And then we'll be very pleased to see you back in class, won't we, Susan? Oh. You're a painter and decorator. Are you? You are. I noticed your hands. Wonderful. You must let me have your card. I've been looking for a proper painter and decorator.'

Ronnie Glover, aesthete, sophisticate, and potential polyglot, with a stub of pencil behind his ear and a fine spray of cream undercoat on his glasses, struck dumb, trying to communicate by the laconic raising of one eyebrow, that his daughter's lack of tap

shoes was due to a trivial administrative cock-up, but going red
instead and dropping a very knock-kneed curtsey.

'Dad?'

'What?'

'What's *bootley gooch*?'

In the late afternoon of a September heatwave, a man, who might have been watering flowerbeds, or sleeping in a deck-chair on his browning, dog-stained lawn, burrowing instead into deep, forgotten layers of garden-shed treasure. A man who knows he will not find a pair of serviceable cricket boots, but cannot stop himself looking. Ronnie Glover.

'Dad? What are you doing, Dad?'

'There's some plimmies in here somewhere.'

'I've got a message for you, Dad. From Madame. She says please can you go and see her about painting her kitchen? And Mum says do you want a cuppa only the milk's gone off but we might have some condensed. You've got to phone her up, and I've got her telephone number. She wrote it down for me. Dad? Are you going then?'

'Eh?'

'To phone her up. You'd better go and do it.'

'I'll do it. Just give me a minute, will you?'

'I'll look for the plimmies.'

'Oh look. A dolly's arm. Is that yours or Gillian's?'

'Don't remember. What do you want plimmies for, Dad?'

'Cricket. Tomorrow afternoon.'

'Where?'

'Dog & Gun.'

'Who with?'

'Your Uncle Vic.'

'Who's Uncle Vic?'

'You know Vic. Off the gang? I've been trying to get your Mum to come. For a bit of an afternoon out.'

'Mum won't go.'

'No.'

'She does the oven on Sunday afternoon.'

'Yeah. Oh. Hold up, hold up. What have we here?'

'Plimmies. You can't play in them, Dad. They're all mouldy.'

'They'll clean up.'

'They're disgusting.'

'They'll clean up. Have you got some of that blanko you had for tennis?'

'Might have. When will you go and phone her, Dad?'

'Later on. Or tomorrow.'

'No, Dad. You'd better go now. She said. She's dead nice. She wears scent, and she can do the splits. She's not stuck up though. She lent Annette a hanky when she had a nosebleed. She's really really nice. Can I come with you when you go round her house?'

'These'll need new laces.'

'I'll get some. And I'll blanko them for you. You get off and phone Madame.'

Ronnie in an airless, fly-blown phone box, with a pile of sixpences, his mind engaged more by a worrying lack of cricket whites than by the business immediately at hand.

'6624.'

'Hello?'

'Hello?'

'Oh. I'm the painter. Ron. Mr Glover. Susan's Daddy. Father.'

'Who is this, please?'

'Hello. I was asked to call Madame. About some painting and decorating.'

'Mrs Granger isn't at home.'

'Oh. Right. Only she wanted me to come and price a job for her.'

'Yes? Well that's what you'd better do then.'

'When should I come?'

'What's the usual time?'

'Monday?'

'Yes?'

'About six?'

'Monday at six. I'll tell my wife.'

'OK, then.'

'Goodbye.'

'Ah, no. Shit.'

'6624.'

'It's me again. The painter. You didn't say where to come.'

'Gartree Road. The Ponderosa. We back on to the golf course.'

The Dog & Gun Sunday XI (The Growlers) against National Savings Bank Second Team, on the Dog & Gun Home Field, two o'clock start. Ronnie, cutting things fine after a hurried roast dinner and words with Eileen.

'Am I glad to see you.'
　'Vic.'
　'You know Malcolm? He's our skipper.'
　'Ron.'
　'How do.'
　'I'm putting you in number 11, Ron.'
　'What, playing?'
　'I'm playing you because Vic's got to umpire because Harry's ricked himself down the allotments. So you're down to play number 11 but you might have to go in 10 because Adcock's guts are playing him up. You can get changed in the Gents'.'
　'I am changed.'
　Glover, R. in plimsolls stiff with whitener, a pair of fawn slacks,

and a cream thick-knit cardigan with a stag on the back.

The Growlers, having lost the toss, going in to field, with Markham (High Class Fruiterer & Greengrocer) to open the bowling from the pig-farm end. Ronnie Glover heading diffidently into the out-field towards an unmarked boundary and a fair, bosomy woman carrying cake tins.

'Hello, pet. It's Ron, isn't it?'

'Yes?'

'Jean. Vic's Jean. You don't remember me.'

' 'Course I do.'

'Where are you off to then?'

'Deep Fine Leg?'

'Well I should think you'll just about do where you are.'

'Yeah?'

'Yeah. See you at tea.'

Dear God, please don't let anybody hit anything over here. Dear God, please let Adcock get better quick, and don't let anybody else get bad guts. Dear God, please let it rain.

The private prayers of Ronnie Glover, as the National Savings Bank Second Team piled on 81 for 3 and Jean Shires' First Team assembled a perfect composition of ham rolls, cheese and tomato sandwiches and homemade Dundee cake.

Should never have let Vic talk me into it. Never again. Just get through this. Tea, and the rest. Then you'll never have to face them again. Apart from Vic. And Pearce. And Norrie Bollocking Chater. Ah shit.

'You all right there, Ron? Got enough to eat?'

'Yep.'

'Your Eileen not coming?'

'She'd got a few things on. Am I still batting?'

'Yes. The Chaters open for us. Then Mal Jessop, Turner, Wildboare, Markham, young Pearce . . .'

'He took a bit of a pasting, didn't he?'

'Well . . . they've got a few on the board, but that's the way it goes. He's all right. He'll do. He just gets a bit lary sometimes with the ball. He's a nice little batsman, mind. Different altogether then. His bowling'll settle down presently, and then he'll be really handy.'

'Adcock won't be fit then?'

'Shouldn't think so. If you have to go in, you can use my bat and pads.'

'I think I've got myself a little weekender.'

'Yeah?'

'Susan's dancing teacher. Big bungalow out on the Gartree Road. She wants a price for her kitchen.'

'Yeah?'

'Only I don't rightly know how much to ask for it.'

'How big is it?'

'Haven't seen it yet.'

'Well you can't price it if you haven't seen it. When are you seeing it?'

'Tomorrow night.'

'There you are then. Have a look at it and then tell her you'll let her know. And bump it up a bit. For Gartree Road.'

'Yeah?'

'Yeah. Chater's padded up. I'd best get out there.'

Ronnie, in the back room of the Dog & Gun, amongst pleasant men in proper cricket whites and pleasant women with damp cloths and tea towels. At the crease, Dad Chater and Bernie Chater, father and son, Dad to face the opening delivery from National Savings Bank's finest. Account opened. One run. Bernie Chater, Parks Department gardener and elder brother to the loathesome Norrie, to face the second ball of the first over.

'No!'

'Yes.'

A mis-field at gully.

'No, Dad!'

'And I said yes.'

Chater, B., run out. Growlers, 1 for 1.

Norrie Chater, with white eyelashes and a smile like a lizard, taking guard at the Lutterworth Road end, pulling to the leg side, and running 2. Norrie's second ball. Another long hop.

'No!'

'Yes!'

'Leave it, Dad.'

'You'll do as I say.'

Chater, N., run out. Growlers, 3 for 2.

Malcolm Jessop, the incoming batsman, having a captain's word with Dad Chater before walking to his crease.

'Did you get enough to eat, pet?'

Jean Shires, emptying tea leaves.

'Yes, thank you. That was a very nice tea.'

'Your wife not here?'

'No.'

'Doesn't she like cricket?'

'To be honest, Jean, I don't know that she's ever watched any . . . I did ask her to come.'

'Ah well. Next time perhaps.'

'I don't know as there'll be a next time. Anyway, she does like her Sunday routine.'

'So do I. I like my Sunday cricket routine. Do the teas. Clear up. Watch a few overs. Maybe do a bit at my knitting. And then a nice drink afterwards.'

'Well that's the other thing. She doesn't really care for pubs.'

'No?'

'And we've got the girls. You get out of the habit, you know, going out together. When they're little you just get out of the habit, and now they're older Eileen's got into her own routine.'

'I don't know what Mal said to Dad Chater, but he's cracking them all over the place. Trying to get back in his good books. You should bring her round some time. Bring her to see what we've done with our lounge since we knocked through.'

'Yeah, Vic's been telling me about it.'

'It's really lovely. It really is. You tell her. You can come round

69

and we'll have a little drink at home. Oh. There he goes. Spoke too soon.'

Chater, Dad, caught for 12. Growlers 24 for 3.

'Hello, Ron.'

Fierce Pearce, shirt too big, neck too thin, Adam's apple dominating all.

'Hello, Pearcie. You'll be on in a minute at this rate.'

'I don't mind.'

'Good tea.'

'Will you get another one when you get home?'

'What? Tea?'

'Yeah.'

'Shouldn't think so. It'll be a bit late for tea, won't it? If we stop for a drink?'

'I don't stop. Not allowed. I'll have my pasty when I get home.'

'You're always hungry, boy. Come to that, so am I. Always bloody hungry. I expect I shall have something when I get home. Ah. See that.'

Jessop, M., caught behind off a half-volley. Growlers 31 for 4.

'Who's in next?'

'Wildboare. Wicket-keeper. What will you have?'

'Sandwich. Bit of cake. Anything really. They'll have kept your pasty for you, will they?'

'Somebody might have had it. But then I can have theirs.'

'Does your Mam put your names on them then?'

Fierce Pearce, fine-tuning his bootlaces, stumped by the question.

Wildboare, clean bowled for 3.

'Bloody hell, Pearce. One more and you're in. Three more and I'm in.'

'Hello, Mrs Shires.'

'Hello, pet. Anybody for a sweetie?'

Jean again, with a score-book, a knitting bag, and a quarter of sherbet lemons.

70

'You do scoring as well as the teas?'

'Not proper scoring. I'm just learning. I mean, I wouldn't really have the time, but I thought I'd get Vic to show me how it's done and then it's handy, say somebody needs to nip to the toilet or something. Go on. Help yourself.'

Fierce Pearce, a relentless scrunching, splattering lemon sherbet demolition machine, circling his arms and stretching his calves like he's seen them do at the County ground.

'You want to watch out for that big bowler of theirs. The one with the sideburns. Vic says he's fast and short, and he says he can turn very nasty. Vic played against him at Kibworth once and he fetched him a very nasty bruise.'

'I shall just hook him.'

'Mm. Or else duck. I don't know why they play Turner. He's took root out there. And another one gone!'

Markham, caught, playing a leg-glance off a good length, followed swiftly by Turner, leg before wicket. Growlers 45 for 7. Pearce and Quinn both eager to get off the mark, and Ronnie facing the inevitable, with a sherbet lemon stuck to his back teeth.

'Now, Ron . . .'

Mal Jessop, a team captain with his work cut out.

'. . . good job you showed up.'

'Adcock no better then?'

'Still pebble-dashing the back of the lav. Still, no worries. Whoever's out there with you, they'll look after you. Probably be young Pearce. You know Pearcie, don't you?'

'Yeah.'

'Let the other batsman call. He'll keep you away from the bowling. Well. The big one with the sideburns anyway. Are they your pads?'

'No. Vic's. He said to borrow them.'

'Yes. Have you got his box?'

'No, I'll be all right.'

'You bloody won't. I shall have your old lady after me if your nuts get mangled. Norrie. Give our man here a lend of your box?'

71

'He can use Vic's.'

'I can use Vic's.'

'No need. There you are. If it's big enough for Norrie, it's big enough for anybody. Is that right, Chater?'

Mal Jessop, laughing more like a machine-gun than a man chasing 81 runs, whose seam bowler Quinn has just been caught by a wall-eyed paper-pusher, without scoring.

'Give us your cardie, pet. I'll mind it. And good luck.'

The longest walk. Walk without end, in plimmies held together by blanko and hope. Two balls to face before the end of the over. Pearce, older than his years, trotting up for a quick conference.

'All right, partner? Don't do anything. Just hang on for two balls and then follow me. Don't look so frit. Think of something nice.'

'Yeah.' *Think of something nice. The Sideburns are coming. This bat's heavy. Think of something nice.*

'How's Mary?'

Mary? What? Pearce? Oh! I did it.

Ronnie's first ball, dabbed to safety. No run. No wicket either. Great.

Think of something nice. Think of Mary. Thanks, Pearcie. Think of Mary. Sideburns. Mary. Mary's sideburns . . .

'Think of dippy.'

'Aaargh.'

And again. Dribbled away into a gap. Safe as houses. Beautiful afternoon. Brilliant afternoon. A time to be amongst good men. Trust, comradeship. Leather on willow. England, my England.

'Oh, well played.'

Fierce Pearce, master psychologist, apprentice house painter, and ascendant all-rounder of the Dog & Gun Sunday XI, slicing and driving the National Savings Bank pace attack into the middle of next week. Growlers 72 for 8. Pearce, 27. Glover, 0.

Ronnie, planning to buy a full set of whites and a smart bag to keep them in. Ronnie, effortlessly fluent in Italian, a genius with brush and pencil, dreaming of a fried egg sandwich with brown sauce, and the rapturous surrender of Mary Tyler Moore.

'Yes! Run three!'

So near, yet so far. A touch of excited nerves. A slip of Pearce's solicitous concentration. Ronnie, at the wrong end of the wicket, in perfect light, with only one ball of the over played. Second ball. Sideburns, taxiing for take-off.

'Leave it, Ron.'

Third ball.

Fried egg sandwich.

'Leave it, Ron.'

Sideburns doing secret things to the ball to make it get up even sharper and hit a tail-ender between the eyeballs and kill him stone-dead.

Esco, esci, esce, usciamo, uscite, escono. Un uovo fresco. Due uove fresche.

Sideburns' malevolent delivery smacked away with a wristy flourish. Four runs.

Who did that? I did. I hit four runs. Runs on the board. Runs on that bloody board!

'Leave the next one, Ron.'

Per piacere, quanto costa un biglietto di andata e ritorno per Milano? Vorrei comprare una maglia rossa per la mia moglie.

National Savings Bank, 81 for 3. Growlers, 79 for 8. Sideburns, lengthening his run-up, taking his time. Ronnie following Pearce's orders, leaving a ball he sensed but never saw. 'Last ball, Ronnie. Just stay put.'

Sideburns, lengthening his run-up still further, trudging towards the pig-farm boundary with his shirt tail flapping, outwards and onwards, over a surprisingly large undulation in the grass, and almost out of sight.

'What a nob-head.'

The voice of Vic Shires? But Umpire Shires doesn't look like he just spoke. Umpire Shires, looking a model of white-coated probity, is now watching the popping crease like a cat at a mouse hole. Sideburns, on his way over the hummock, his full-length appearance presaged by a thundering deep in the earth and a scattering of frightened sparrows. Retribution for four measly runs on its way in the shape of a mean, mardy-arsed Sunday cricketer from Desford.

Mary. Fried eggs. Bums. Pears. Quanto costano queste fragole *Nine sevens are sixty-three* . . .

A little flurry of traffic on the Lutterworth Road. The Dambusters' March being whistled through the wicket-keeper's teeth. And . . .

'Ayeeee Yah!'

The climactic cry of a spent but confident bowler.

'No ball.'

Umpire Shires, deadpan, remote.

'Ah no! Does that mean I've got to face him again?'

'Just one. Hang on, Ron. Ron! Quick! Get behind it!'

Sideburns, delivering himself of a full toss off the shortest run-up in Dog & Gun cricketing memory, and Ronnie Glover making inadvertent contact, skying it in the approximate direction of third man, but on a trajectory for Mars.

'Where is it?'

'Where's it gone?'

'It's in the tree.'

'Can you see it?'

'No. But it's in the tree.'

'Lost ball.'

Vic Shires, moving swiftly to confer with Umpire Sedley and press him to decisive unanimity.

'Lost ball?'

'Lost ball.'

'Lost ball be buggered. Let me through. I'll fetch it down.'

Dad Chater, eager to re-establish good will by climbing the elm tree and returning with the ball.

'Get down, you silly old sod. We're not letting you break your neck here. Your Bernie wants to do it when he gets you home.'

'I've never heard anything like it. Fetch another ball.'

'Lost ball. And the tree counts as 6. So that's Growlers 86 for 8 including extras. Bails off and everybody into the boozer.'

'How about that then?'

'Yeah. You done all right.'

'I was bricking myself, lad.'

'No, you done all right. Third highest scorer. No, fourth highest.'

'Yeah?'

Ronnie, acknowledging the applause of Jean Shires, Muriel Wildboare and Beverley Jessop, with bashful pride, returning through lengthening shadows to the Lords' Pavilion, England cap doffed, and the sole of his left plimmie flapping with each step.

'Here we are, here we are, here we are again . . . fit and well . . . feeling as right as rain. Never mind the weather, now we're all together . . .'

Ronnie, wobbling homeward on his bike on a September night warm enough for shirt sleeves. Seven pints in his belly. Stag motif cardie in his carrier bag. Joy in his heart. 10 not out, and the Growlers wanted him back. Well Vic and Pearce and the skipper did. He'd had a grand tea and a skinful of ale, and he'd had a Sunday, nearly a *whole* Sunday without having to humour Ma or Eileen, or threaten Gillian. And now he was tired. The nice kind of tired when you just want a cup of cocoa and a slice of bread and dripping and then sleepybyes. He was on his way home from the pub, all on his own, and the Ten O'Clock Horses weren't after him.

*W*hen a house is just called The Ponderosa and it hasn't got
a number, how do you arrive at it? If you haven't got a motor? Do
you leave your bike up at the gate? Or get off it and wheel it up to
the front door? Or the back door even? Buggered if I know.

Ronnie Glover, going for the Wheeled To The Front Door
option, but faltering at the very last and making an apologetic jab
at the bell-push. The distant, futile barking of two small dogs.

*Hello, I'm the painter. No. Hello, Ron Glover, the painter and
decorator. Ron? Ronald? Bloody hell, Glover. She's only a dancing
teacher. She's not royalty.*

'Hello. You're punctual. Do come in.'

Jacqueline Granger in an ordinary blouse and skirt and little
flat shoes and no lipstick, looking normal and tired, and bollock-
achingly beautiful.

'Did you find us without any trouble?'

'Oh yes. No trouble.'

'Come through and I'll show you what we need doing. Actually,
we need everything doing. It's not that it's scruffy. The place is

only a couple of years old. But the people we bought it from . . .
Well, we just like different things. So we'll be decorating all the
way through eventually. But the first thing is the kitchen because
its depressing the hell out of me. Come and have a look.'

Ronnie, still on the doormat, wondering about his shoes.

'No, no. Please come through. I've just made coffee. Will you
have some?'

Kitchen. This is what she calls a kitchen. Like in a magazine.
Pictures on the wall. Two sinks. Rotary spice rack. And a terrazzo
floor. Clean. Cool. Does Madame clean kitchen floors? 'Oh yes
please.'

'How would you like it?'

'However it comes.'

Ronnie, peering into his first ever black, sugarless coffee.

'Now look. This colour has simply got to go. It's so chilly, and
this room looks north as it is. So I want sunshine in here. Don't
you think?'

'Mm.'

'Yellow, or peach. Something to persuade me I'm doing the
ironing in Amalfi.'

She does ironing. 'Yellow would be nice.'

'It would, wouldn't it? I thought that. It would look pretty with
all my blue china.'

'I've brought some shade cards. I can leave them for a day or
two if you like?'

'Oh no. Let's get on with it. Let's look at them while we have
our coffee and you can help me choose.'

'Won't you want to ask your hubby?'

'Christ no. The only thing he ever comes in here for is ice cubes.
No. Whatever we choose will be fine by him.'

So this is Madame. All these nice plates, and bottles of wine.
Perhaps she's a lush. But books. Books in a kitchen. Fanbloody-
tastic.

'That's nice.'

'Yes.'

'Or that.'

'You don't want to go for a pale lemon?'

'No. I want sunshine. I want the yellowest yellow you can find.'

'Looks like this one then?'

'Beautiful. I love it. When can you do it?'

'It'll have to be evenings. Or the weekend.'

'Can you start tonight?'

'Well not really . . . the paint . . . I shall have to . . .'

'I'm kidding. Whenever you like, but the sooner the better. I'll give you a key. And I'll give you some money, to get the paint and whatever else you need. And I'll give you some more coffee. Pass your cup.'

'I see you're a bit of a reader.' *Prick. What a fucking stupid thing to say.*

'Mm? Oh those. Those are cookery books. I'm a bit of a reader and a lot of a cook. You won't have had dinner. Can I get you something?'

'No thanks. I've been home. I've had tea.' *Dinner.*

'Susan's enjoying her classes.'

'I know. She talks of nothing else. Madame this, Madame that. No, she really loves it.'

'Are you a dancer?'

'No. Not a step.'

'Not ballroom?'

'No. It's not a thing we ever did. I believe my Dad did. I can do the Twist. Do you want the ceiling kept white?'

'Um. Ceiling. Yes, I think so. Do you think so? Now how about if I give you twenty pounds today, to get things started, and then either you can tell me when you need more, or you can give me a bill at the end?'

'Well, usually . . . well, whatever suits you. I mean, twenty'll cover it. Everything.'

'What labour and things?'

'For the kitchen, yes, everything.' *You could have got more.*

'Wonderful. I like leaving things to an expert.'

'So I'll go tomorrow, to the Trade Counter. And if I can get the colour you want, I'll make a start tomorrow night. I'll wash it down, but I won't start painting if the light's bad.'

'Whatever you say. Here's a key. I'll be teaching 'till eight tomorrow and Tony's away, so just let yourself in. And help yourself to drinks or anything you need.'

'Thank you very much. Isn't that lovely. Whatever are they?'

Ronnie examining a watercolour above Madame's fridge.

'Figs. Yes, they are lovely.'

'Figs?'

'Have you ever had them?'

'I've had Syrup of Figs. And Fig Rolls.'

'Well that's what they look like when they come off the tree. You cut them open and eat the insides. They're red, and slightly juicy, with lots of seeds. People go wild for them, but personally I prefer just looking at them.'

'Very nice. All right. I'd best be off then.'

'OK. When I get back from class tomorrow, I'll show you round. Show you the other rooms we want to do, so you can start helping me with colour schemes.'

'Right you are.'

'Will the dogs bother you?'

'Do they bite?'

'I can't promise. I'll shut them away. Or I could take them with me. That might be better. What do you think?'

'I do like dogs. We've got one at home.'

'I'll take them with me.'

'Whatever you think is best.'

'And what am I supposed to call you?'

'Eh?'

'Am I supposed to call you Mr Glover while you're painting your way round my house?'

'Oh. Right. Sorry. Ron. I'm Ron.'

'All right, Ron. And I'm Jacqueline, but you can call me Jack. Everybody else does. See you tomorrow, all being well? *Ciao*.'

Ciao. Ciao! *Figs. And books in the kitchen. Twenty crisp folding ones, and the front door key, and a beautiful, smiley woman with legs up to her shoulders and dark, dark hair that moves. Jack. Oh Jack. All this, and the cricket, and the girls are all right, and Eileen's happy because she's giving the bedrooms a good bottoming. Thank you, God. Oh Thank You.*

'Once, at Chatham barracks, just after I'd joined up, they asked for anybody who spoke a foreign language. Any foreign language at all. I've always wondered, if I had have done, you know? And ever since then, I've thought about doing it. Learning something. That'd really be a turn-up for somebody who left Medway Street School on his fourteenth birthday. See, there's a lot more to the world than they showed us at Medway Street, and I'd like to have a look at it. I'm not saying it's all better than we've got. I just want to have more of a look and decide for myself. I'm not a snob, Eileen. I'm not being awkward, or trying to make you feel inferior.'

'I don't feel inferior. But I'm still not asking for figs.'

'I only want to have a look at one.'

'I don't care.'

'I'll go myself. I'll ask Markham from the Growlers.'

'You do that.'

'Are you happy, Eileen?'

'How do you mean?'

'Well . . . are things how you want them to be. You know? Do you feel you're getting what you want out of life?'

'I hope you're not manœuvring for what I think, because I've got my visitor, so you can forget that.'

'No, no. I didn't mean that. I'm just trying to talk to you. Trying to explain, about doing the Italian and everything. See, I'm not doing it to get on your wick or make you feel left out.'

'I don't feel left out.'

'Good.'

'Why should I feel left out?'

'Well sometimes, if a person tries to better himself, it upsets people, because they think maybe they're not good enough for him any more.'

'I wouldn't call doing Italian bettering yourself.'

'No. All right. Broadening your horizons, say. Educating yourself. Tasting new experiences.'

'I am *not* asking for figs.'

'No.'

'I wouldn't call doing Italian bettering yourself. I'd call getting a spin-dryer bettering yourself.'

'So are you happy? You've still not said.'

'I'd call boxing the bannisters in bettering yourself, or getting a little car.'

'Vic and Jean want us to go round. He's built a bar in the corner of his lounge. I said we'd go.'

'When?'

'Don't know. When would you like?'

'You go.'

'No, they said both of us. Jean's nice. She said to bring you round.'

'I don't know.'

'What's to be said against it?'

'We go there, they'll expect to come here.'

'So?'

'I'm just saying. They'll expect it. You never think, Ron. You're

83

going to have to start thinking before you open your big mouth.'

'Eileen . . .'

'What?'

'Nothing. How would you like your kitchen done yellow?'

'It's green.'

'I know. So how about yellow, for a change? Only I might be coming by some yellow paint. A lovely sunny yellow to make you feel like you're doing the ironing in Amalfi.'

'Right. That's it. If you can't talk sense, I'm going to sleep.'

'Please yourself. I'm going to go to Vic and Jean's. And I'm going to try the yellow. *Gialla. Una cucina gialla.*'

'I'm not listening.'

Eileen, who used to be pretty and still could be if she didn't look so moithered all the time, lying neatly, back turned, eyes closed, dead set against newfangled colours in her kitchen. Eileen Glover, née Barlow, virgin bride of Ronald Glover, at St Andrew the Less, 1 December 1946, four weeks before he got demobbed, in his petty officer's uniform and looking very handsome. Eileen, who loves Ronnie in the quiet, dutiful way Barlow women love their men, and who would have liked Susan to have been a little boy because that would have been nice for him, even though he's always maintained he was tickled pink to have another little girl. Eileen, who *is* happy, but doesn't hold with silly talk.

'T here's no demand for it.'

'There is now. I'm demanding it.'

'Don't you get like that with me, Glover.'

Ted, of Walters' Paint & Wallpaper Trade Counter (nineteen years, man and boy), who has not yet heard that the customer is always right.

'You can order it, can't you?'

'Depends. How much are you buying?'

'Two quarts.'

'No chance. I'm not doing a special for less than a gallon.'

'Ah, come on, Ted. I don't want a gallon.'

'Take it or leave it.'

Take it. Jack wants it. Eileen doesn't. Take it. 'For tomorrow?'

'Shouldn't think so. End of the week more like.'

'I thought this was a bloody paint shop?'

'Are you ordering this stuff, Glover, or are you going to fuck off?'

'I need it tomorrow. I've got a customer waiting for it.'

85

'Take another colour then. Take Buttermilk. Tell them it comes out lighter than the shade card. They won't notice.'

'Order it.'

'What?'

'Order Sunburst. Two quarts.'

'A gallon.'

'Thursday latest.'

'Friday. Cash on delivery.'

'I'll pay now. Deliver it to the job. Are you ready? It's to go to The Ponderosa, Gartree Road. For Mrs Granger. Have you got that? Oh, and put, *If no-one in, leave in porch.* Let me see. Ponderosa, you bonehead.'

'That's what it says.'

'No. It says Pongderosa.'

'Same thing. It's off *Bonanza*. The Pongderosa.'

'Now don't let me down. You've had your money, so Friday, and no cock-ups.'

'If it comes, you'll get it. If it don't, you won't. I couldn't give a monkey's. Oi, and Glover?'

'What?'

'I hate your bloody guts.'

*N*ow what? Go round there. Leave a note. No. Have tea. Then *go round. Leave a note, or wait for her. No point in shifting stuff and cleaning down. Not yet. Bugger. Could leave a note and then go back later to make sure she's got it. In case it's fallen down the back somewhere or one of the dogs has had it. Don't be a prat. Those dogs couldn't reach a note if you left it somewhere sensible. You'll see her soon enough. Stop behaving like a prick. Making up reasons to go round there. Tuesday. Shepherd's Pie, cabbage, tinned peas, and Instant Whip.* 'Eileen, where's the writing-paper?'

'Don't know as we've got any. What do you want it for?'

'I shall have to leave a note for Madame. I can't get her paint till the end of the week.'

'I've got some rough paper, Dad. I'll give you some. Can I come round with you when you take it?'

'No. Better not. Are you sure we haven't got any Basildon Bond, Eileen? We ought to have something.'

'Why? We never write to anybody.'

'Well what do you use when you have to send a sick note up the school?'

'I don't know. I've got a little pad somewhere.'

'Where? That's what I'm asking for, woman. A little pad. Where is it?'

'I don't know. Susan, have a look in the tablecloth drawer.'

Ronnie, eating his Shepherd's Pie, too hot, moving it around fast with his mouth open, putting more salt on, tasting nothing.

'Oh no. That's lined, Eileen. You don't write letters on lined paper.'

'Why not?'

'You just don't.'

'It's only a note from a painter. She's not going to expect a coat of arms on it. Gillian, stop mashing everything up.'

'Why? It all gets mashed up inside you.'

'Just do as your mother tells you and eat it in separate bits. I'm going down the shed.'

'What about your Instant Whip?'

Ronnie, happy suddenly, and impatient, because he has remembered his lovely drawing paper, and in his head he is composing a letter to the most beautiful woman in the world.

'*Dear Jack, Unfortunately . . . Sorry for the delay . . . Have had to order your paint specially . . .* No. Write it how you'd say it to her. How would she say it? Jack, *Bit of a hold-up with the tinned sunshine, but it will be here by Friday. Please send a message with Susan if Friday doesn't suit. Ron.* Yeah. That's it.'

*D*eep joy. To let yourself in and know you can stand as long as you want in the hall and have a good look. Just the hall, and then straight into the kitchen. Wait for her to show you the rest of it. She'd know. If you had a peep anywhere else, she'd know. You can smell people, even when they've just passed through. This house smells of her. Like lemons and coffee, and a bit doggy too, but not as bad as Gums. Which one was the kitchen? On the right, definitely. No. Oh, look at that. A little bog and a washbasin. Like a little cloakroom, with coats hanging up and old shoes. She comes in here before she takes her dogs out. There might be something in a coat pocket. A hanky or something. There'd be no harm. She'll expect you to have been in here. No. Don't even think about it. Even if you look the other way and have a quick feel in the pockets, you're still doing it. It's still deliberate. It'd be nice to have something though. Don't do it. She's trusted you with a key. So don't, don't, don't do it. Just take the note into the kitchen, have another look at the job, and then go. Yes.

Ron, in Jack Granger's kitchen, smaller and more cluttered than his first impression. Dishes in the sink. A bottle of wine with the cork shoved back in. The *Daily Telegraph*, yesterday's and today's. Ballet shoes under the table, long and curved with darning on the toes.

She'll have done some practising. Last night, after I'd gone. And then had a drink, and probably a bubble bath. She was all on her own. Then this morning she'll have come down here in a white silk thingy and had freshly-squeezed orange juice and a French croissant.

Ron, choosing the best place to leave his note, avid for the pictures and cookery books and the bills and postcards pinned to a cork board, and anything else to help fill in his picture of Jack which is still excitingly sketchy; failing to notice though, that the unwashed dishes spoke of bacon and eggs with brown sauce, and a mug of Typhoo tea.

T he door unlocked, but no-one home. Tea towel folded over the grill hood of the cooker. Pristine oven glove hanging from the oven glove hook. *Radio Times* safe inside the leatherette *Radio Times* cover. All in order, except for the cushion squashed down in Pop's armchair.

'He's in here.'

The Duchess of Ashby de la Zouch, in crimplene slacks and a fluffy jumper, hailing Ronnie from the door of her bungalow, across the shared path.

'He's in here, dear. Mrs G's at the Seniors' Club. Come on in and have a drink.'

'I was only passing. It's nothing special.'

'Come on in anyway. We were just going to have another little drink. Come in. Don't be shy. Any son of Archie's is a friend of mine. Go on. Go through. I'll fetch another glass.'

The Duchess's living-room, unrecognizable as the twin to Ma and Pop's polythene-wrapped world. Cushioned, swagged and draped in uterine folds of velvet. The Magicoal burning needlessly for a hot September. And Pop, on the floor, with a bottle of Emva Cream and a jigsaw of *The Fighting Temeraire.*

'Son?'

'You look hot.'

'I'm snug.'

'Where's Ma?'

'Seniors'. Were we expecting you?'

'No. I had to come up to Gartree Road about a job, so I thought I'd drop in.'

'Good thing Beryl spotted you.'

'Sherry all right for you, Ron? We've been busy on my jigsaw. Can I get you a little sandwich?'

'No, you're all right, thanks.'

'Little chicken sandwich? Bit of ginger cake? Archie? How about you?'

'I wouldn't say No to a chicken sandwich. If it's no bother?'

' 'Course it's no bother. I love having somebody to make a sandwich for. This is my wallpaper I was telling you about, Ron.'

'Very nice.'

'Little bit of salad with your chicken, Archie?'

'Go on then.'

'Ma stopped feeding you?'

'She left me something. I lobbed it in the bin. I'd sooner come round here and do the jigsaw.'

'What time's she due back?'

'Not yet. They're having Housey-Housey. She's a lovely person, you know? Beryl. Very generous and kind and lovely.'

'How many sherries have you had?'

'Don't you look at me like that.'

'I'm not looking at you like anything.'

'Yes you are. It keeps me going being able to slip round here for a little drink and a laugh. I reckon God looked down and he thought, that poor bugger Archie Glover hasn't had much of a life, fifty years cutting shoe patterns and coming home to that old scowler. I'll send him Beryl. That bungalow next door's coming up vacant presently, as soon as Annie Goodyer has tripped over that stupid rug, bust her hip and died of pneumonia. I reckon that's how it went. Sent to me by the angels.'

'There you are, my darlings. Oh, hold on. I know what you'd like with that. A little bag of crisps. Do you need a hand up off that floor?'

Beryl, pulling Pop back from the brink of tearful indiscretion, with a plate of chicken sandwiches, and then, with a tender stroke of his few poor strands of hair, pushing him over the edge.

'You're a very lovely woman, Beryl. Sent by the angels. And I don't care who hears me say it.'

'Saturday then?'

'Yeah.'

'Come for a bit of tea and then we can have a few drinks later. Bring the girls.'

'Smashing.'

Ronnie, agreeing to the plans of his good mate Vic without any idea how he might bring these things to pass. Saturday teatime Eileen would be looking forward to soaking in the bath till her legs turned red and then a nice long read of her *Woman's Own*. Susan would be on her way home from Beginners Tap. He might be painting Jack's kitchen. How to get everybody on a bus up to Vic's in time for a ham salad without Armabloodygeddon occurring? Impossible.

'Tell you what, Vic. We might be a bit pushed to get there in time for tea. Susan has her dancing Saturdays.'

'Make it later then. It's all the same to me. Only don't bother eating. Jean likes to do a spread.'

'Yeah? All right.'

Ronnie, experiencing the relief of someone who is completely
out of trouble, instead of the lingering anxiety more appropriate
to a man who still has a lot to square with his wife.

'Vic.'

'Yeah.'

'How old would you say, how old would most men be, roughly,
when they give up the old whassisname?'

'Pace bowling?'

'Nah. You know? Leg over?'

'Dunno. Varies I suppose. Jean's got a brother, Ed, he's early
forties and he's never got started. Never done it. Whereas Charlie
Chaplin, he's never stopped, has he?'

'You don't think that's all got up by the papers?'

'Can't be. If a bloke's still getting women in the family way, he's
got to be still doing the business.'

'Suppose so.'

'I'd say it all depends on the state of your health. I mean,
if you're shuffling about on a stick or you've got bad breathing,
you're not going to be thinking about rumpy, are you? Well, you
might be *thinking* about it, but that'd be as far as it went. You're
always going to think about it, aren't you, because first thing of a
morning there he is, the old feller, giving you a wave. But if you've
got stiff knees, well . . .'

'Suppose. And it'd depend on the woman as well, wouldn't it?'

'Certainly.'

'Because they dry up, don't they. After they've finished having
kiddies, they sort of close up.'

'I don't know. I have heard something about that. What's all
this in aid of anyway? You shutting up shop?'

'So you don't think a man and a woman of say, about seventy,
for argument's sake, you don't think there'd be anything to worry
about?'

'Well he's not going to get her knocked up.'

'No.'

'He might have a nice time trying though.'

95

'Yeah? No, you're kidding me.'

'Who is this man and this woman for argument's sake then?'

'No, no. I was just wondering, that's all.'

'Don't give me that. Come on. Not your old folks? Get away. Are you worried you'll be getting a baby brother? Worried you're going to have to share the family heirlooms?'

'No, don't talk daft.'

'What then?'

'You'll never breathe a word?'

'Never.'

'Cross your heart?'

'And hope to die in a cellar full of rats.'

'Well. It is Pop. I don't know anything for certain. But it is Pop.'

'I thought he was a bit badly, your Pop?'

'He is. Breathing. Waterworks.'

'Don't sound very likely then.'

'No? But they've got a widow moved in next door, wears lipstick and likes a drink, and he's forever round there. The minute Ma's back's turned he's round there.'

'No. He's just looking for company. He must be bored stuck indoors with bad waterworks.'

'I don't know.'

'Well has he said something? Something must have set you off thinking?'

'Well . . .'

'Yeah?'

'It's just a couple of times. I've seen them. Touching.'

'Get away.'

'I dropped in Tuesday night and Ma was out at Seniors. I found him next door, drinking sherry and doing her jigsaw.'

'And touching her?'

'No. Tuesday it was her touched him. Stroked his hair, like. But I have seen him touch her. I've seen him put his hand on her bum.'

'Well I'll be jiggered.'

'I mean, it's not the kind of thing, you know . . . ? Is it?'

'It's in the bag.'

'You reckon?'

'Hand on bum? No question. So he's not so poorly as you thought?'

'Well that's the other thing. See him at home, he's like a corpse. See him with Beryl and he's all pink and sweating. I think it's his heart.'

'I think it's his heart and a few other bits as well.'

'And what if he pegs out while he's round there?'

'Nothing you can do about it, bonny lad. If I was you I'd turn a blind eye and hope he dies a happy man.'

'Aaargh, Shires. It's disgusting.'

'Only because he's your Pop. I think it's bloody marvellous. I hope me and Jean are still at it when we're seventy. You've cheered me up, Ronald. Really cheered me up. Now. Priming window frames or glossing front doors? Toss you for the glossing.'

Thursday. Sausage, beans and mash, *Z Cars*, and Susan practising 'We're a Couple of Swells' on the kitchen floor.

How to do it? Float it as a faint possibility? Ask if she wants to? Tell her it's all fixed up and Jean's ordered extra milk? Best thing. Only wait till she's properly into Z Cars *and then slide it in fast.*

'Where's Gillian?'

'Out.'

'I'm starting Madame's kitchen tomorrow night.'

'Mm.'

'Should finish it by Monday.'

'Mm.'

'Vic and Jean want us to go round this Saturday. I said I'd have to ask you.' *Slippery, lying bastard.* 'But I said most likely we would.' *Light blue touch-paper and retire.*

'Yeah. All right.'

'You don't mind then?'

'I don't want to go, but if I say No you'll only get in an egg.'

'I won't.' *Careful.* 'If you really don't want to go, we won't go.'
What a pillock.

'No. We'll go.'

'Great. You'll like Jean. Everybody gets on with her. And Susan can come. See their new lounge. Have a drink, listen to their Hi-Fi. It'll make a nice change. Pick Susan up from Tap and then catch a bus up there. It'll do us good to get out together.' *Enough.* 'We don't have to stop late.' *Shut it. Christ Almighty.*

'Ron.'

'Yep.'

'I'm trying to watch my programme.'

Ronnie, out early on the fine autumn morning of the Friday he's been waiting for, cycling away from the direction of work and the doors he must paint before he can see Jack and turn her kitchen Sunburst Yellow, to the parade of flat-roofed shops where Markham (spin bowler, Dog & Gun Sunday XI) is just setting out his cauliflowers.

'Ay up.'

Blank.

'Ronnie Glover. I was your last man in against National Savings Bank.'

'Ay up, chap. How're you going on?'

'Not so bad. You're open then?'

'If you're buying, I'm open.'

'Right.'

Ronnie, feeling surreptitiously through his loose change and wondering what an apple might cost.

'No. I was just wondering. About figs. Do you ever get them at all?'

A slow, regretful sucking in of breath by Markham, who has been called as an expert witness, but has mainly bad news to deliver.

'I have seen them.'

'Yeah?'

'Down the wholesalers.'

'Yeah?'

'But I don't stock them. Nobody does. You'd never shift them.'

'No?'

'No.'

'What becomes of them then?'

'What?'

'The ones they've got down the wholesalers?'

'Hotels.'

'So I'm not likely to get one?'

'How many would you want?'

'Don't know. I was hoping to get a look at some. Just to get an idea. How come people won't buy them?'

'Bit of an acquired taste. Foreign, you see. I find customers feel a lot safer with bananas.'

'But you have tasted one?'

'No. Wouldn't care to. Any road, I don't think you could just take a bite out of one. You'd need to turn them into jam. They're probably on the bitter side. Or sour.'

'I'd heard they were very nice. But I only wanted to have a look. I thought they'd make a nice painting. A nice picture.'

'I'd heard you lot painted ceilings and windows. How about apples? Apples makes a nice painting.'

'Go on then. I'll have two bob's worth.'

'Good man. Are you playing Sunday?'

'Shouldn't think so. Adcock's fit. Might come though. Might come and watch if I'm not working.'

'Right you are then. See you.'

'See you.' *Brilliant. Late for work. No figs. And two bob wasted on manky apples.*

'Oi, chap.'

Markham, running after him, with something dark and lustrous in his hand.

'I don't know if it'd be of any help, but if you wanted something exotic, these are getting very popular.'

'What is it?'

'Avocado pear.'

'What do you do with it?'

'Cut it open, take the stone out, and put a bit of salad cream in the hole where the stone went.'

'Yeah?'

'Savoury, you see? Not sweet, even though it's called a pear. Getting very popular at your better class of wedding reception.'

'Well I never.'

'Go on. Try it.'

'I haven't got any more money on me.'

'You can owe me.'

'Tell you what. You have the apples back and I'll have this.'

'Done.'

'With salad cream?'

'With salad cream.'

'Cheers mate. And if you should come across any figs, remember, I'm your man.'

'Y ou deal with her, Ron, because if you leave it to me I shall probably kill her. Go on. Take your belt to her.'

'That's not the answer.'

'That's right. Make a muggins of me. Well if you won't do it I will.'

'Eileen. Calm down. We will deal with it. But belting her's not the answer. She just wants keeping in for a week or two, or something like that. She stops in tonight and then we can sort it out later on.'

'No, Ron. Not later. Now.'

'But I've got to get off round Madame's.'

'I don't care.'

'What about tea?'

'There isn't any. How can I make tea when I've got troubles like this?'

'Eileen, my guts think my throat's cut.'

'So take your belt to this little madam and then I'll make you a sandwich.'

'Sandwiches are no good. I've been grafting all day on sandwiches, and I'm going to be grafting all night. This is all your fault, young lady. What have you got to say for yourself?'

Gillian, jaw set, eyes defiant, slumped in a chair, picking, with chewed, stubby nails, at a tear in the trim of Rexine piping.

'Well?'

'What?'

'What have you got to say for yourself?'

'Nothing.'

'Why did you do it?'

'Felt like it.'

'*Felt* like it? How can you feel like doing a thing like that?'

'There weren't nothing else to do.'

'Rubbish. Life's full of things to do. You could have read a book, or took the dog for a walk.'

'Or helped me.'

'Yeah, or helped your Mum. You were offered the dancing classes and you turned your nose up at them. Whatever did you do it with?'

'Needle.'

'Well it looks terrible.'

'It's my arm.'

'You realize that could go septic?'

'Serve her flipping right if it does.'

'You'd better put a plaster over it. Keep it clean and covered up. And you're to stop in. You stop in tonight, all the weekend, and all next week.'

'You can't do that.'

'I bloody can, girl. You've upset your mother, and if she's upset, I'm upset. You've had too much leeway, so now I'm pulling you up sharp. Understand? Understand?'

A voice made tiny, so it might be argued its words didn't really count.

'Yes.'

'Louder.'

'Yes.' *Stupid git.*

'Now you'd better go and put some Dettol on it and get it covered. And don't forget, you're to be inside these doors every night until I say different. You want to get yourself something to do. Do a bit of sewing. Or drawing. You used to be good at drawing. Remember when you used to draw Popeye?'

Gillian, remembering, caving in. Defeat and misery, with a lingering trace of truculence, riffling across her face like cards being shuffled in a pack.

'Come on. There's no need for crying.'

Ronnie, catching hold of her in a brief, embarrassed hug, a young woman with heavy white legs and a look of bovine stupidity. His daughter. Who used to be a wiry, rebellious little tyke, always doing deals on comics and Lucky Bags, always answering back, especially her Mum. The Mum she's all but turned into.

'Go on. Go and find some Dettol.'

'She should have had a belting.'

'I've dealt with it. All right?'

'No, it's not all right. I'd have given her a belting. I suppose you realize she'll be scarred for life?'

'It'll fade. What's it say anyway?'

'Rick.'

'Who's Rick?'

'Another good reason for you to take the strap to her.'

'Get us some tea, Eileen.'

'Get your own tea.'

'Actually, have we got any salad cream?'

'Try looking.'

'Where do we keep it?'

'With the sauce.'

'Yeah?'

'Sideboard.'

'Right. It couldn't be anywhere else?'

'No.'

Ronnie, hungry enough to eat anything, even a slice of one of his Ma's marmalade tarts, whacking a little pile of tomato ketchup into the hollow of an unripe avocado pear and wondering what his next move should be.

'Whatever have you got there?'

'Avocado pear. Markham gave it me.'

'That's horrible. Get it out of my kitchen.'

'They're the latest thing at wedding receptions. Leave it on the side. I'll have it later.'

'I don't want it left on the side. I don't like it. Ron. Take it with you and chuck it. Ron. Where are you going?'

'To Madame Granger's via Barry Road chippy, and don't expect me 'till late.'

Ronnie, closing lines of communication with a snap of his bike clips. Gums, on his hind legs, flickering his tongue at the sauce on the avocado pear, with his eyes on Eileen, prepared for a fast getaway.

Cod and Six. Or Pie and Six? Pie'd be better. Less smell. No chips'd be best. Two pies, one peas. Or a battered sausage. It all smells. Just setting foot in a chippy, you've got the smell on you. In Jack's house, that'd stand out a mile. What do you smell like anyway? Nothing cooking at home. Paint? Soap? Clean. Quite nice. Better really to eat afterwards, on the way home. Or, to not actually stand inside the shop. Stay outside, get them to bring your order out, eat it quick and then let any bit of a smell waft off while you're biking round to Jack's. That's it.

Ronnie, smelling of Palmolive, dog, and linseed oil, standing in the doorway of Fryer Tuck's, trying to attract the attention of a big hard-faced blonde.

'What?'

'Can you do me double Pie and Peas and bring them out to me?'

'You what?'

'Double Pie and Peas please, but brought out.'

'Are you taking the piss or something?'

'No.'

'We don't do bringing out.'

'I wouldn't ask, only I don't want to get the smell of chip fat on me.'

'Can't hear you.'

'I don't mind paying a bit extra.'

'Push off. Go on, before I fetch my old man out of the back.'

'You all right there, Renee?'

A small, shiny man with batter on his hands emerging through the curtain of plastic streamers. Ronnie, cycling away fast, unfed, misunderstood, not waiting to inspect the cut of Fryer Tuck.

A door closing, with a bang. Poodles yodelling.

That was the front door. She's here. She'll smell the paint and come straight through. Keep painting. Pretend you didn't hear. Any minute. Funny. She must have gone to the bog. Maybe somebody was in all along and then they went out. No. Couldn't be that. Best put your head round the door and see. Just say How Do and then get straight back to the painting. 'Hello? Anybody there?'

From across the hall, a voice.

'Who the hell is that?' and then a figure, carrying post and a letter knife, tall, greying, in a dark blue suit and a perfect but manly skin.

'Sorry. I'm the painter. I'm doing the kitchen.'

'Oh yes. Of course. Fine. Yes. Carry on.'

'Ron Glover.'

'Yes? Oh, yes. Fine. Tony Granger.'

'Madame said to just let myself in and get on with it.'

'Fine, fine.'

'Only I was hoping that was her, when I heard the door. To see if she's happy with the colour, before I do any more.'

'Jack's in London. Back tomorrow. Or Sunday.'

A nauseating lurch of disappointment.

You're not going to see her. She just wants you to paint her kitchen and then clear off out of it. 'Perhaps you could have a look at it? See if you think it's what she had in mind?'

'Wouldn't have a bloody clue, frankly. House is Jack's department.'

'Well I'll just finish the bit I'm doing and then I'll be out of your way. I thought I'd come tomorrow. If that's all right?'

'Whatever. Just put some of those little Wet Paint jobs up if there's anywhere I should avoid.'

'Come and have a look. It's just the yellow that's wet, and that's drying fast. You'll be all right by morning. See? Do you think it's what she wanted?'

Tony Granger, hovering on the threshold of his own kitchen, stripped of self-assurance. 'No idea. Probably. If it isn't, Jack won't hesitate to say. Care for a drink, at all?'

'I have had a cup of tea. Madame did say . . .'

'No. A drink.'

'Thank you very much.'

'Take water with it?'

What's the answer? 'Just a drop.'

'Let you put your own in. Need to let those fucking dogs out for a leak and then do something about food.'

Ronnie, belly responding with a growling roll to the trigger-word, eyeing the whisky in his glass.

'I can finish now. Fifteen minutes and I can be out of your way.'

'In your own good time.'

The dogs again. The door again. Silence.

That's the kind of man a woman like Jack has in her life. A man who wears cuff-links and drinks Scotch while he's opening the gas bill. That's what you'd have to be to have a woman like Jack. Empty your brush, dickhead. Leave her kitchen nice in case she comes back tonight after all. Do a good job. Maybe get asked to do a few more. Take her money. Go home to Eileen. Dream of Mary Tyler Moore.

'Just off?'

'Yeah. I've left you straight, and I'll be back about nine in the morning. Or later, if you like?'

'Yes. Whatever. Probably be playing golf.'

'About nine then?'

'Out. Come on out, you stupid fucking animals.'

A scrabble of poodle curls on the back seat of the Rover. Tony Granger, no jacket, tie still beautifully knotted, standing with a large white parcel in his hand.

'Sorry? Yes. Nine. Any time. Definitely. Can't hang about. Chips are getting cold.'

The dinner ladies of Southfields Secondary Modern sitting down to meat loaf and rice pudding with jam as the school falls asleep for first period, Monday afternoon.

'Do anything nice at the weekend, Joyce?'

'Not really. My daughter came, with the grandchildren.'

'That's nice.'

'Not really. They're little sods. If I know they're coming I nail everything down.'

'Ah, into everything, are they?'

'Everything. And it's not nice, Lilian. They've broke more stuff of mine than ever my own three did. See, my Pat, she switches off. She walks through my door and parks her backside and she switches off. Bum on the settee, shoes off, telly on. They're running riot and it all washes over her.'

'That's a shame, isn't it, because it's not the kiddies' fault. Still, you wouldn't be without them?'

'Oh no, I wouldn't be without them.'

'You do anything nice, Anne?'

'No. We went down the Conservative Club, Saturday night.'

'Oh well, we know how you finished up then.'

'I hope you had your frilly drawers on.'

'Conservative Club means she had her frilly drawers *off.*'

'I did not. I had my old Aertex on. Don't make no bloody difference once they're round your ankles.'

The raw, unfettered laughter of women who know they will not be overheard. Joyce, whose husband has prostate trouble and a very demanding vegetable garden. Connie, widowed five years, who'd give anything for the sound of her Albert's snoring. Anne, who reaps the aphrodisiac harvest of Brylcream and best suit most Saturday nights. Lilian, who lives with her Mum, and laughs with the best of them even though she can only guess at Anne's life. And Eileen, who doesn't think the way Anne talks is very nice, and who has had a very exciting weekend indeed.

'We went out Saturday night. Visiting friends. They've got ever such a lovely home. I wish you could see it. It's just like in a magazine. Will be. When it's all done.'

'Oh yes?'

'Vic and Jean. They're very good friends of ours, and what they've done is, knocked through, where it used to be a front room at the front and a living-room at the back, now it's all one big room with fitted carpet and two settees. And, hold on till you hear this, they've got their own bar. Bottles up on optics, beer-mats, cocktail cherries, everything.'

'My Pat had a bar but one of the kiddies rode his tricycle into the front of it and it all collapsed. It was only like cardboard.'

'What's the idea behind it? You might as well go to the pub.'

'It's like having your own pub, only no pushing to get a drink, and no rowdies.'

'And no chucking-out time.'

'Vic and Jean, our friends, they've got Full Frequency Stereophonic Sound as well. They've got this record of a train, and it's just like it's going through your living-room.'

'What do they want that for? Why haven't they got music?'

110

'They have got music. They've got music as well. It's called a demo disc. And I'll tell you something else. They've got a carpet in their bathroom.'

'If we had a bar at home I'd never get past our front door on a Saturday night. Eh? No Conservative Club. Just the bedroom ceiling.'

'Do you ever get a Saturday night off, Anne?'

'Oh yes. Say, if he's had a near miss on the pools, or if his back's bad. He's not a sex machine, you know? Least ways, that's what he tells me. I said to him, "Are you sure?" '

'Actually, we may be going to knock through. We were talking about it last night. You see, with Ron being in the trade, he could easily do it.'

'Your Ron's not a builder. You have to know about girders to do a job like that.'

'Yes, but being in the trade, he knows a lot of people. We could easily get it done.'

'I don't know that it's a good thing. I like having a front room. At least you know then you've got somewhere decent to sit if anybody comes. I won't let Pat's kiddies in my front room. I've threatened them.'

'We've got a front room.'

'I've still got a bed in my front room, from when Albert . . . you know. It can stop there as far as I'm concerned. I never go in there. Never dust it or anything. I've lost all interest. I like my back kitchen with my little wireless and my knees up the chimney.'

'If you knock through, Eileen, how are you going to go on with your girls? If they need to be swotting, or when they start courting? You don't all want to be on top of one another, telly on in one bit, record-player going down the other end.'

'Well we're just thinking about it. We're definitely going to carpet the bathroom though.'

'Oh no. I shouldn't like that. Because when men go for a tinkle they splash it all over the place. You'd have the smell of it in the carpet all the time. Like cats. I like somewhere you can swab down. I mean, let's face it, a man having a jimmy couldn't aim it down the Mersey Tunnel.'

'But you have a pedestal mat. That's what Jean's got. A little towelling mat that can go in the boiler every Monday. Well I think it's nice. Very modern. Vic's a scream. He's got a little Vauxhall so he said he'd run us home, no trouble. So I sat in the front because Susan was tired and she wanted her Dad in the back with her, and all the way home Vic kept singing "Oh let me take you home, Eileen". I mean it should be *Kathleen*, but you've got to laugh.'

'You do anything nice at the weekend, Lilian?'

'I did. I made a bit of chutney. And then we walked to the postbox and posted my sister's birthday card. Not too far because Mother's not been so good, but we saw some lovely gladdies in somebody's garden. Really lovely. So that was nice.'

Eileen Glover, not going straight home, although she has left a tablecloth soaking and it is her week for windows. Eileen, going to the Co-op to look at carpet samples, and Widdowson's Fashion Fabrics to look at skirt lengths, and ending up, though she hadn't really planned it, standing in Woolworth's trying a Calypso Orange lipstick on the back of her hand. A woman of thirty-six, carrying a little too much weight and a hairstyle she's had since 1954, selecting Rimmel Iridescent Eye-Shadow in Ice Blue, Outdoor Girl Creme Foundation in St Tropez, a bottle of Amami setting lotion, ten spiked rollers, and a Gala lipstick called Frosted Macaroon. Twelve shillings and ninepence.

I shouldn't really spend that much. Go on. When do you ever spend anything on yourself? Always last in the queue at home. Always getting little things for the girls. Jean says, If you look nice you feel nice. And she does. Lovely and jolly and still looking nice. Nearly fifty probably. And it wouldn't be twelve and ninepence every week. A lipstick lasts years.

'Are you buying these or what?'

A thin, insolent girl called Carole, an Easter-leaver from

112

Southfields Secondary Modern, who wants no truck with faded old dinner ladies.

'Yes I am. And I'll have a jar of Nivea as well and don't you be so cheeky, Carole Monk.'

Eileen Glover, tail up, hurrying home with a bag full of goodies and a plan to become more like her new friend Jean.

'Oh, sorry. Wrong wife. I thought I lived here but I must have got the wrong gate.'

'Mum's all poshed up, Dad.'

'Susan! I have got the right house. I thought I had and then I clapped eyes on this film star that's stood here slicing beetroot and I thought I must have wandered into Sophia Loren's place by mistake. That's the trouble with these semis. They all look the same.'

'Will you stop messing about and get washed?'

'Eileen. It is you. Oh my duck. You tell me who did that to you and I'll go and sort them out.'

'She's got eye-shadow on, Dad.'

'Is that what it is?'

'Well?'

'Well what?'

'What do you think?'

'I think I'd sooner have piccalilli than beetroot.'

'Ron?'

'No, I'm sorry. You look lovely. Very very different.'

'Yeah?'

'Yeah. So what's brought this on?'

'Just fancied a change.'

'Aunty Jean wears blue eye-shadow, doesn't she, Mum? Madame wears greeny-brown.'

'You bought all this, did you?'

'Yes. Any objection?'

'Not at all.'

'You spend enough on your drawing pads and your Italian stuff.'

'No, I said. Not at all. So this is my new look Eileen?'

'Could be. Haven't decided if I like it or not yet.'

'I like it, Mum.'

'I might have to tell Mary Tyler Moore I'm seeing another woman. Where did you buy it?'

'Woolies.'

'Do they sell anything to make your legs grow all the way up to your armpits?'

'Cheeky beggar.'

'Eileen?'

'What? Get off.'

'No, let me whisper.'

'What's he whispering, Mum?'

'Seeing as how you're looking so glamorous . . .'

'Get off.'

'How about, you know?'

'Susan, go and shout Gillian for tea.'

'Eh? How about it?'

'Get off. And stop it. Susan'll hear you.'

'Is that a definite No or a maybe?'

'It's a No. Can you get the top off this vinegar?'

'Why is it No?'

'Because it's Monday.'

'That's daft.'

'Because I say so.'

'I don't see the point of it in that case. If you didn't do all this for a bit of attention, what was the point of it?'

'Gillian says she's not hungry. Dad? Mum says we're going to knock through and have a big long lounge like Uncle Vic and Aunty Jean. Are we, Dad?'

Ronnie, eating cold, fatty lamb and mash with beetroot bleeding into it, trying to be pleasant and normal.

'Are we, Dad?'

Stupid ugly cow. I didn't want to anyway. Not with you. 'I don't know, darling. It'd be a big job. I couldn't do it on my own.' *She looks like a clown. Her hair's all lopsided and she's not done the back at all. It's all flat at the back.*

'Uncle Vic's nice isn't he, Dad? And Aunty Jean.'

'Yes. They're very nice.' *I hope to God nobody sees her looking like that. You're a cruel horrible bastard. She's tried to do something different and all you can do is pick holes in it. You should be encouraging her. Making some suggestions without being obvious. She means well. She always means well. I hate her. She's a lump. I bloody hate her. I want a woman like Jack. I want Jack.*

'Lamb all right, Ron?'

'Smashing. Pearce is off sick. Sprained ankle.'

Ronnie, struggling with a pair of blunt nail-scissors and a shaving mirror. Breath from the very nostrils he is trying to tidy up misting the glass and adding to the problems of working on a reflection. Ronnie tapping on his daughter's bedroom door.

'Gillian?'

'What?'

'Are you decent?'

No reply.

'Gillian?'

'What?'

'Can I come in?'

No reply. Ronnie, waiting too long, then opening the door like an apologetic child.

'Gillian? Have you got any tweezers?'

'On there somewhere.'

A nod in the direction of dressing-table clutter. Hairspray cans. Bottles without tops. Tops without bottles. And a dusty tangle of plastic snap-together beads.

'Can't see them.'

'I might have lost them.'

'Well can you have a look?'

'God!'

The most perfunctory of glances.

'No. I've lost them. What do you want them for anyway?'

'I've got a splinter.'

'Let's have a look.'

'No. It's in my foot. Not to worry. How's your arm?'

' 'S all right.'

Gillian, rolling over with her magazine, presenting her back to her father, signalling that his time is up.

Down the stairs with quiet nonchalance.

'Don't forget you've got to fetch Susan.'

'I haven't forgot. I've just got a few things to do first. Anyway, I don't know why you can't go.'

'Because I've got to get this zip put in.'

'What's the rush?'

'So my dress is finished and I can wear it on Sunday.'

'What's Sunday?'

'Cricket. I told you I'm coming. I'm helping Jean with the teas.'

'You don't need a new frock to do cricket teas.'

'I only want to look nice. Don't you want me to look nice?'

Eileen, in snuff-coloured terylene and still too much eyeshadow, wheedling jokily. Bent over her dressmaking, putting pins between her lips to hold them, deaf to Ronnie's reply, blind to his rummaging through his tool bag and his rapid exit, upstairs, with his paperhanger's scissors concealed along his forearm.

Success. Nostril hair and eyebrows trimmed. Swift supplementary shave and a splash of Corvette. Breath checked by breathing air into cupped hands and sniffing.

'That'll have to do, my old son. Probably won't see her anyway.

118

She probably didn't like the kitchen. Or she wishes she hadn't been so friendly. Ah, bollocks. Best to get down there and find out. Put yourself out of your misery. She should have liked the kitchen. It did look nice.'

'Dad! We're doing a panto and it's *Cinderella*, and I'm being a mouse, and a fairy helper, and a confetti.'

'Are you? That's nice. Did Madame say anything?'

'Yeah. She's having a meeting of all the Mums to tell them about the costumes, and if anybody misses more than two rehearsals they can't be in it any more.'

'She didn't say anything about her decorating?'

'Don't think so. I bet Cinderella's dress'll be brilliant. We haven't started the mouse dance yet because that's tap. We're starting that on Saturday. I love *Cinderella*, don't you, Dad? Dad? Can we get chips?'

Ronnie, re-tying his shoe laces quite unnecessarily, to gain a few more seconds before leaving.

'Have you got everything? We don't want to get halfway home and find you've left your cardigan or something.' *Come out of that door, damn you. Come out and speak to me.* 'Is Madame busy in there?'

'She's only talking to the lady that plays the piano. You

120

can go in if you want to. You're allowed.'

'I was just wondering whether she liked her kitchen now it's finished.'

'Go in and ask her. Go on. I'll go.'

'No you won't.'

Too late.

'Madame. My Dad's here to fetch me tonight.'

Ronnie, hanging back, then stilled by the sight of Jack, one leg raised on the barre with her body folded comfortably over it, and then, at the sound of Susan's voice, unfolding, black skirt, black legs, black jersey criss-crossing her chest, hair caught in a pair of tortoiseshell combs to keep it off her handsome face.

'Ron! I wanted to call you, but I didn't have your number. The kitchen is divine. Quite wonderful. But I must owe you some money. Have you brought your bill?'

'No, no. We're all straight moneywise.' *Ask for another ten.* 'You paid me before I started, remember?'

'Yes but that was for materials. I don't think it can have been nearly enough for everything. Let me give you a cheque.'

Oh fuck. 'No, please. I'll just stick a nought on the end next time.' *Ah God, look at that smile on her.*

'Well next time will be different because it'll be the sitting-room and we shall need wallpaper and things. So we must talk about that soon.'

Soon? When's soon? 'Whenever you like.'

'But the other thing is, our pantomine.'

'Yes, Susan said.'

'Well it's going to be quite a big thing. We're doing *Cinderella* and the Am Drams are going to take the main parts and we're going to do the dances and choruses. It's very exciting, and we're going to need all the help we can get.'

'Dad'll help, won't you, Dad?'

'I do hope you will.'

'How do you mean?'

121

'Scenery. Painting it. Making it. You'd be very clever at it, I know you would. Can I put your name down?'

'I've never done anything like that.'

'I'm sure you have. Say you'll do it?'

'Yeah? Yeah, fine.' *She fancies you. She bloody fancies you.*

'And if you've got some friends who could help? And Susan's Mummy? The more the better because there's going to be such heaps to do.'

She doesn't fancy you. She just wants her scenery painted. 'I'll see what I can do.'

'Good. And we must talk, very very soon.'

'Yep. Right.' *Tell her you're not on the phone.* 'I'll wait to hear from you then.' *Tell her. It doesn't matter. She already knows you're a peasant.* 'Send a message with Susan. That's probably best.'

Jacqueline Granger, withdrawing now, changing her shoes, putting on a jacket, jangling keys, establishing, in the nicest possible way, that the conversation has ended.

'See you on Saturday, Madame. Me and Dad are going to get chips.'

'How's the frock?'

'It's not a frock. It's a dress. And this material's been a pig to machine. It keeps slipping and sliding all over the place.'

'Well don't bother putting your machine away when you're done because it sounds like Susan's got a few jobs lined up for you. She's in a panto.'

'See, this was what I said would happen, didn't I? Before she started these dancing classes, I said it'd be all expense and I've got to have this and I've got to have that.'

'It won't be all that much. Madame's going to let the Mums know. And she's asked me to do the scenery.'

'You can't do scenery.'

'Yes I can.'

'When you see Vic tomorrow I want you to ask him to tell Jean I'll be bringing two dozen butterfly cakes on Sunday.'

'You don't need to come, you know?'

'I want to come.'

'You've changed your tune.'

'No I haven't. Jean specially asked me.'

'I specially asked you the first Sunday I played for them and you said you were too busy.'

'So?'

'So how come you're suddenly not too busy?'

'Oh, so you don't want me to come now. Now I'm making a special effort, you want me to stop at home.'

'No. I'm just saying. I mean Christ Almighty, Eileen, tell me the last time you didn't spend Sunday afternoon with your head in the oven? Eh? When was the last time on a Sunday afternoon that we didn't have to go out of the front to get round the back because you've got the oven pulled out, blocking the door, going over all the shiny bits with the Dura-fucking-glit?'

'Keep your voice down.'

'You're a mystery to me.'

'I just thought of a way round it, that's all.'

'Yeah?'

'I won't clean the oven.'

'I've waited seventeen years for this.'

'We'll have salad.'

'What? On a Sunday dinner?'

'Yes. Then the oven won't get messed up.'

'What, no roastie?'

'No.'

'Are you feeling all right, Eileen?'

'Yes. Why?'

'Eye-shadow and new frocks and no Sunday roastie, all in one week.'

'Something bothering you?'

'No. But you don't even like cricket.'

'You don't know what I like.'

'Anyway, Jean's in charge of cakes.'

Susan Glover, in red trousers and a cardigan with daisies down the front, walking all the way to Glebe Crescent without stepping on pavement cracks, dead leaves, or nasty flubbery things spat out by old men. Breaking into a run at the sight of her Grandad.

'It's our Susan. Hello, my duck.'

'Hello, Grandad. I'm in a panto.'

'Lovely. I shall come and see you. Say hello to Aunty Beryl. This is the lady as lives next door to me and your Grandma now.'

'Hello.'

'Hello, darling. Which panto are you in?'

'*Cinderella.*'

'Oh, that's my favourite. Are you Cinderella?'

'No. She's one of the grown-ups. I'm doing three dances. I'm being a mouse in the kitchen. That's tap. And then I'm being a fairy helper when the pumpkin gets changed into a coach. And then I'm being confetti for the wedding. Those are both ballet. Are you really going to come and see it, Grandad?'

'Definitely.'

'And I shall.'

'There you are. That's two seats gone already. Near enough sold out.'

'What are you doing?'

'I was just doing a bit of weeding between these flags, and then Aunty Beryl opened her door to shake a duster and we got chatting.'

'What's Grandma doing?'

'She's indoors. You want to go on in and see her? I'll be in directly.'

'But before you go, Susan, tell me what you'll be wearing for your fairy dresses. Is your Mummy making you something nice?'

'Yeah, I think so.'

'Well I've got some special bits of material that'd make lovely fairy outfits, and if they'd be any use, you can have them. I've got blue and pink, and peach, I think. So you tell your Mummy. Try and remember to tell her?'

'Yeah.'

'You can come in and have a look at them, if you like. They're only in my bedroom cupboard. Couldn't she, Archie? She could come in and have a glass of limeade, and have a look for herself.'

'I think I'd better go in and see my Grandma, actually.'

'Yeah. You do that, my duck. And tell her I'll be in in a mo. Say bye-bye to Aunty Beryl.'

'Bye.'

Nothing cooking. Parazone from the sink meeting Devon Violets from the bedroom, and the background warble of *Sing Something Simple*. Ma Glover, bolt upright in her chair, with a tight grey face.

'Hello, Grandma. I've come to see you.'

'Your Dad not with you?'

'No. Only me. I'm going to be in a panto, Grandma, and you and Grandad are going to come and see it.'

'Is he still out there pretending he's weeding?'

'He's talking to the lady next door.'

'Fetch me a Rennie, there's a good girl.'

'Have you got a bad tummy?'

'Heartburn.'

'Shall I get you a glass of milk?'

'No. Just a Rennie. Where's your Dad got to this morning?'

'He's in his shed. He's doing drawing I think. We're having salad today because Mum's going to cricket with Dad. Last Saturday we went to Uncle Vic and Aunty Jean's and Aunty Jean told Mum she ought to come and help with the cricket teas and take more of an interest. Dad's got the hump. He says it's too cold for salad today.'

'I haven't seen your Mum in nearly a fortnight.'

'She's making a dress. It was meant for summer really but she's going to wear it with a cardigan. It'll be all right. God, you should see Gillian's arm. It's all swelled up and there's yellow stuff coming out of it. Will be when she squeezes it. And she's not even going with Rick any more.'

'What's wrong with her arm?'

'She scratched Rick on it and now she's not even going out with him. She's going with Andy now. Grandma, how do you feel somebody up?'

Ma Glover, eyes closed, lips pursed in preparation for an alarming sideways shift of her dentures, and then a pat of the back of her head.

'I had a perm on Friday.'

'It looks nice. Mum said she might get a perm. And she might learn shorthand and typing and get a job as a secretary. Mum says we might knock through as well and have a big long lounge like Uncle Vic and Aunty Jean. I might be a secretary. Or a ballerina. Or a doctor.'

'You want to go into the Shoes. You can get good money. Or the Hosiery, like I did.'

'No, I think I'll be a ballet teacher.'

'Listen to that old fool out there.'

127

The sound of Pop's laughter and the Duchess's chatter over 'De Camptown Races' on the wireless and the fast, delicate ticking of a little foldaway clock.

'He's talking to that lady called Beryl. Gums got out again last night. Dad says he's in love with a spaniel in Featherstone Drive and he's going to have to have his nuts cut off. What are you and Grandad having for your dinner?'

'We'll have a bit of ham later on.'

'When we went to Uncle Vic and Aunty Jean's we had bacon and tomato pie and Peach Melba. Then we had records on and drinks from the bar. I had Tizer. Uncle Vic let me put the records on because they haven't got any children. Mum says some ladies haven't got any eggs. Because once a month there's supposed to be an egg, and if the egg meets the seed you get a baby, and if it doesn't the egg dies and it all comes away with blood and stuff, and you get a terrible bellyache and you have to take sanitary towels to school with you. It's called Having Your Visitor. Or Menstruation. But some ladies haven't got any eggs. They're just born like that. So they don't get babies. Have you ever had bacon and tomato pie, Grandma? It's lovely.'

Pop's face at the window suddenly, mouthing through the glass.

'Aunty Beryl says would you like a choc-ice?'

'No, better not. Got to go home for dinner in a minute.'

Pop, mouthing again.

'Are you sure? We're having one.'

'No. I'm talking to Grandma.'

'Old fool.'

'She's nice, isn't she, Aunty Beryl? She said she's got something I can have for my panto costumes. Shall I get you another Rennie?'

'No, I shall be all right if I sit quiet.'

'Grandma, what do you do all day long?'

'I find plenty to do, don't you worry.'

'Yeah, but. There's not much hoovering to do is there? Do you go out for walks?'

'Sometimes.'

'You should come to our house. You never come to our house.'

'I go to Seniors.'

'What do you do there?'

'Bingo. Sing-songs. There's a chiropodist comes once a month.'

'Chat to your friends?'

'Yes.'

'Who's your best friend, Grandma?'

'Oh I don't know.'

'Who do you sit next to?'

'Different people. Mrs Orr.'

'Is she your best friend?'

'It's not like that when you get old. You don't want to get too pally. Some of them don't know what day of the week it is. Some of them are on their last legs.'

'Is Mrs Orr on her last legs?'

'She had a bad fall last winter.'

'Have some of your friends died?'

'Annie Goodyer died next door.'

'Were you sad?'

'Didn't really know her. Mr Saunders. Mr Farmer. Mrs Savage at Seniors. They all died.'

'Were they your friends?'

'Mrs Savage was doolally. Never really spoke to the others. You can't speak to the men or you get the evil eye from their girlfriends.'

'What? They have girlfriends at Seniors?'

'Fancy women. Fussing round men. Trying to get another husband. Buttering them up. They die anyway. Everybody dies. Specially the men.'

'I don't want my Grandad to die.'

'What time's your dinner?'

'I've got to go in a minute.'

Pop, in the doorway from the kitchen with a silly smile on his face and a flake of chocolate on his chin.

'Fancy you not wanting a choc-ice.'

'I was talking to Grandma. She'd got indigestion so I fetched her a Rennie. She's nodded off now.'

'No I haven't.'

'I've got to go anyway, Grandad. We're having salad.'

'Are you? I'm glad I'm not coming round your house for dinner then. Gillian all right?'

'Yeah. Mum says she's a little slapper.'

'Mum and Dad all right?'

'Yeah.'

'Want some pocket money?'

'Yes please.'

'Half a crown do?'

'Thanks, Grandad.'

'Half a crown for you, half a crown for Gillian?'

'Thanks, Grandad.'

'And don't forget to put us down for that panto. Front-row seats, mind.'

Susan Glover, taking leave of her Grandma, her Grandad, and the plummy chummy voice of *Two-Way Family Favourites*.

'Hello and welcome. This is Jean Metcalfe in London, and waiting to join us from Cologne, I hope, is Bill . . .'

'It's going to be a terrible squash, you do realize?'

'No it won't. Two in the front, two in the back.'

'There'll be five of us. Six if Susan's coming. You're forgetting Pearce.'

'I thought he couldn't play?'

'He can't. But he's still coming.'

'Well Susan's not. Anyway, it's not far. We can squeeze up for ten minutes.'

'And cake tins as well. The main thing, Eileen, with a cricket match, is getting your players there with all their kit. Not cake tins. What's Susan going to do then?'

'She's drawing costumes for *Cinderella*. Gillian's going to make them a sandwich. Here's Vic and Jean, so shut up now. I don't want you creating an atmosphere.'

Ronnie and Eileen, pressing into the back of Vic Shires' Vauxhall Velox for the four-mile drive, one either side of Pearce with his support bandage, a carpet slipper, and a big excited smile.

'I might bat, Ron.'

'You can't bat on a bad ankle.'

'He might have to. We might be a bit short. He can bat with a runner. Well, Eileen, looking forward to your first cricket tea? You're looking very stunning if I may say so. Very summery. It's a pity we haven't got better weather for it.'

'I hope you're going to be warm enough.'

'Jean's usually got her long coms on by the end of the season.'

'Who's coming then?'

'Can never say till you're there. I can tell you who's not coming. Quinn. He's got too much marking or something. And Turner. He's covered in bruises. Fell downstairs.'

'Upstairs.'

'What, pet?'

'He fell upstairs.'

'Right. So that's two we're short for a start-off. You all right in the back? I want you to be gentle with young Pearce, Eileen. I don't want you dropping any of them rock cakes on his good foot. Oh dear God in heaven, look at this. They've come in a bus.'

'That can't be them.'

'It is. I recognize some of them. There's that bloke from Croft that's got a plate in his head.'

'There's hundreds of them.'

Metal Box Sports and Social Old Contemptibles, players and supporters, filing off their hired coach in immaculate whites and caps quartered in claret and blue.

'Is that a bad thing, Vic?'

'It's bloody marvellous. We can borrow as many as we need. You might not need to bat after all, Pearce.'

'I shall be all right, Vic. Look, it's hardly swollen at all now.'

'It'll be up to the skipper, lad.'

*　　*　　*

132

Final match of the year. Metal Box Pensioners against the Dog &
Gun Sunday XI, on Lutterworth Fox Cubs pitch, behind the Sir
Frank Whittle public house (use of pavilion till seven-thirty only).
Ten minutes to start time, four men short, plus Pearce's ankle.

'Where's Bernie?'
  'He's had to go to Warwick to see the wife's mother.'
  'Where's Adcock?'
  'He is here, but his guts are bad again.'
  'What's the plan then?'
  'We're borrowing.'
  'How many.'
  'Many as we like. If Harry's not here, are you umpiring again?'
  'Can do.'
  'Right.'
  'And Pearce is willing to bat with a runner.'
  'Right. Here's what we do. Can your mate run?'
  'Glover? Yeah. Wouldn't you do better borrowing a runner?'
  'What, a pensioner? No, Glover can run. So I'll open with
Norrie Chater. Then Dad Chater 3, a foreigner 4, Wildboare 5,
Markham 6, foreigner 7, Pearce 8, foreigner 9 and 10, and then
Adcock.'
  'How about the bowling?'
  'Markham. Adcock, if he's still breathing. Me. And one of theirs.
Or Glover. Can you bowl, Glover?'
  'I used to a bit. But I haven't, not in years.'
  'Well go and turn your arm over for five minutes and see how
you go. I might put you on later.'

The Growlers, having lost the toss, put in to bat, aided by four
tightly-coiled match-fit volunteers from the Metal Box camp and
plenty more where they came from should the need arise.
  Norrie Chater, out from under his stone, with a fine powder of
plaster dust on his hair, ready to face the deadliest weapon in the
Metal Box arsenal, The Grunter. A maiden over. Mal Jessop, a

man who doesn't enjoy his Sunday cricket as much as he used to, a man whose wife has just told him, over a nice piece of topside, another month gone and still she's not pregnant, Mal Jessop to face another of Metal Box's finest, The Tryer. A bowler who appeals, on principle, three times per over, and always does it with conviction. Six wides.

'I brought some butterfly cakes.'

'Did you? So did I. Bev, I hope you haven't brought butterfly cakes. They'll all be sprouting wings.'

'I brought veal and ham pie and some tins of dressed crab. I couldn't be bothered with baking.'

'Are you all right? Bev? Chater's out.'

'I'm a bit down.'

'Are you? See, what we do, Eileen, we do the sandwiches now and wrap them in damp tea towels. Set the cups and stuff out. Then, about ten to four, we put the water on for the tea and put the cakes out while it's coming to the boil. What's the matter then, Bev?'

'Oh I dunno.'

'You need a holiday.'

'We can't leave the shop.'

'No. It must be hard. Eileen, let me get you an apron. I should hate you to get marge on your new dress. See this, Bev? Eileen made it herself. And you've done your hair different, haven't you?'

'Well I thought I'd have a crack at it.'

'What's Ron say?'

'Not much.'

'No?'

'He's not interested in that kind of thing. I could dye it green and he wouldn't notice. He's always got his head in a book. Always down the shed.'

'He's a one-off, your Ron, isn't he? Deep waters. Does Malcolm care what you look like, Bev?'

'He does and he doesn't. He won't let me have my hair cut.'

'Do you want to get it cut?'

'I wouldn't mind. I couldn't though. He'd go mad. He'd smash something if I did.'

'What? Mal?'

'Oh yes. He's got a terrible temper.'

'Well I am surprised. He always seems so steady. He never seems to change. That's old man Chater gone. How many's on the board? 23. 23 for 2. Not bad. They've got one of the borrowed ones going in next. Excuse me. Excuse me. What's the name of the batsman that's just coming in?'

'Jervis.'

'Is he any good?'

'Don't know. He's somebody's uncle.'

'He's got quite a walk on him. Quite a swagger. You didn't do a fruit cake then, Bev?'

'No.'

'Who's winning?'

'Too early to say, Eileen. Are you not familiar with cricket? See, our side is batting at the moment. Then we'll have tea. Then the other side'll be batting. We're doing all right, but it's early days yet. Oh. Well he didn't last long. We can have another look at that walk of his.'

Jervis, out to a straight delivery from his nephew.

'Sit out on the steps and watch for a bit. We can manage in here. Watching's the best way to learn.'

'Why isn't Ron out there?'

'Because he's batting lower down the order. In fact he's not batting at all today. Pearce is going to bat and Ron's going to run for him, to save his ankle. See, Bev's Malcolm is out there at the moment and that's Wildboare going out to join him. He'll be facing the next ball.'

'And he's one of ours?'

'Wildboare? He's our wicket-keeper. He's married to Muriel

135

and she'd usually be here doing teas but she's had to go in for a little operation.'

'We should have got her a card.'

'We should.'

'And what do we do after tea?'

'Clear up and then watch.'

'What time does it finish?'

'Six fifty-five sharp. Then we go for a drink.'

'I'm thinking about doing shorthand and typing, did I tell you?'

'Yeah? Do it. Why not.'

'I thought I'd see about night school.'

'You don't need to, you know? You can teach yourself. You'll waste that much time at night school, fiddling around, people coming in late, and asking stupid questions. You could borrow my typewriter and teach yourself.'

'Yes, but what about the shorthand? You have to go to classes to learn that.'

'I didn't. I made it up.'

'How do you mean?'

'Well I went for this job. It's a long time ago. Coronation year. And I told them I could do shorthand, so every time I was supposed to be taking a letter I just got it down as best I could, did my own abbreviations. It's not hard. And they're all much of a muchness anyway, business letters. Anyway, one day, I'd been there quite a while, more than a year, Sidney Fox, he was my boss in them days, he said to me, "Jean, I don't know what I'd do without you but however did we come to take you on with no shorthand?" He said he'd realized the first time I did any letters for him because what I typed up wasn't exactly what he'd said. But he said he never minded because what I typed up was always better.'

'Fancy.'

'There goes the skipper. No. Hang on. Well look at that. Did you see that?'

Mal Jessop, survivor of an unexceptional ball from the

136

Grunter, chopped onto his own stumps but failing to move his bails.

'That was lucky.'

'Was it?'

'That was the luck of the devil.'

'He'll be out next ball.'

'Will he?'

'Yeah. He'll bring it on himself. He's a very pessimistic man really.'

'No. He's going to prove you wrong.'

'Well he won't be long, I'll bet you. I can tell by his shoulders.'

'Yes, I know what you mean. With Vic it's his chin. If something's bothered him and he's not saying, he holds his chin funny. Eileen, do you want to put the kettles on, pet? There he goes. You were right about that then, Bev.'

Jessop, hooking an absolute sitter to cover. Dog & Gun 47 for 4. Markham on his way out to join Wildboare, and the gas lit under the water for tea.

'I didn't see you doing much.'

'That's because I never got to bat.'

'I'll come and sit with you after we've cleared up. If all you're going to be doing is sitting around.'

'I'm not going to be sitting around after tea, am I? We'll be fielding after tea. Jesus Christ, Eileen, I wish you'd try and get the hang of it a bit better.'

'Don't you snap at me. And mind your cup. You're tipping it.'

'Ay up, chap. I've got something for you.'

Markham, purveyor of manky apples and patchy spin bowling.

'What? Figs? Did you get some?'

'I'll just get my bag.'

'Ah brilliant. Cheers mate. I'd given up on them to be honest.'

'Well. I seen these and I thought of you.'

'Yeah?'

From the darkness of Markham's kitbag, a small crumpled paper bag that does not promise ripe, curvaceous figs. One fig? A fig leaf?

'There. How about them?'

'What are they?'

'Nuts.'

'Still in their leaves, like?'

'Yes. Kent cobs. I thought of you. I thought they'd make a nice painting.'

'Right. Thank you very much.'

'They look nice, don't they? Straight out of a painting.'

'They do.'

'How did you go on with the avocado pear?'

'Not bad. Very interesting. I didn't paint it. But I had a little taste of it. Very different.'

'I sell melons, you know?'

'Yeah?'

'I come by all manner of things.'

'I suppose you do. So, how much do you want for the . . . ?'

'Kent cobs?'

'Yeah.'

'No, have them. On the house.'

'That's very kind.'

'Glad to help.'

'Thank you.'

'I have got a ceiling needs papering, if ever you're at a loose end. Wouldn't take you five minutes.'

'Well I've got plenty on just at present, but, you know, if it slacks off . . . Pearce? What's up, lad? You look like you've lost a quid and found a gum boil.'

'Mal should have put us higher up the batting. We should have had a go.'

'Yeah, but it's maybe for the best, lad. It might have set your ankle back. Better if you rest it and get it properly better.'

'It is better. Look, I can hop on it.'

'Don't hop on it, you pillock. Have you had enough to eat? Here, have another butterfly cake.'

'I'm going to practise really hard this winter, Ron.'

'Good for you, Pearcie. And you're coming to the pub after. You'll have to if Vic's running you home. Did you tell your Mam you'd be later?'

'Forgot. I wonder why there isn't any fruit cake today?'

Adcock and Jessop to open the bowling against Metal Box. 64 for 5 the target. Ronnie Glover sent to field at roving deepish fine leg, on standby for a change of bowler if Adcock gets an urgent call of nature, along with Markham, Turner, who showed up during tea, and Leadbetter and Bicknell from the Metal Box supporters' bench.

First wicket, at the cost of 11 runs. A mighty off-drive from their opener with the purple nose, caught by Norrie Chater at third man. Metal Box powering through the teens and twenties, into the thirties, on veal and ham pie and the wisdom of age. Then, two catches in the slips. Jessop on a hat trick, his shoulders revealing signs of temperament, but only to his wife, chucking it away, offering it for a crack to the long-on boundary where Chater Senior is lighting a roll-up.

'Bastard.'

'Language.'

Umpire Shires cautioning the Dog & Gun captain and losing his place in the over.

'Was that four balls or five?'

Metal Box 48 for 4 courtesy of a catch by Wildboare that will be talked of for many years to come.

'Oh! What! See that, Eileen?'

'What?'

'That catch. Did you miss it? See, Adcock bowled an out-swinger and Wildboare went to go that way for it but the batsman got an inside edge to it and Wildboare managed to get right across and catch it. That was brilliant. He's like a chimpanzee. I wish Muriel could have been here. What a little star. I think your Ron's coming on. Yes. Adcock's running off and Ron's coming on.'

'What's he going to do?'
'Bowl, you chump.'

Glover, bowling for the first time in thirteen years, pacing out his run-up, wishing he had practised more and that his wife wasn't sitting on the pavilion steps in a homemade frock and lopsided hair.

All you do is run a bit, turn your arm over and let go the ball. You've done it plenty of times before. When you were a kid you used to do it even when you hadn't got a ball. I've forgotten how. You can't forget. It comes back. Ah, sod it.

A maiden. Hallam (retired foreman, Metal Box) startled by the pace of the Dog & Gun's new bowler, hopping and tapping defensively, wondering at the fire-power of such a mild-looking man in horn-rimmed specs.

'Well bowled, Glover. You had him rooted to the spot.'
'Well bowled, Ron. Did you know he could bowl?'
'No.'
'Vic won't be very pleased. Well he will, if the Growlers do all right, but he won't like Ron being a better bowler than he is.'

Metal Box 51 for 4. Glover's second over.

Same again. You can do it. Don't even think. Just do it. Ah Jesus, what's Eileen doing? Waving at me? Fucking waving at me. Concentrate. Parlai, parlasti, parlo, *something, something,* parlarono, *something, anything . . .*

The ball rearing violently and pitching on the off, taken one-handed by Jessop.

'Do you work, Beverley? Only I do school dinners, but it's really getting on my pippin. It's the same old routine every week and then you get home and you've got to start again. Some days I think if I have to look at another potato I shall scream.'

141

Glover's second ball of the over, launched with the aid of the past definite of *essere*, getting up smartly and hitting the middle stump clean out of the ground. 53 for 6.

'Good man, Ron. Good man.'

'Now I wouldn't mind being a secretary or something like Jean, but I don't think Ron'd let me. It suits him the way things are. Me being home to get his tea and see to the girls.'

'You do realize you're married to a bit of a hero out there, do you, Eileen? You're yacking away in here and nobody's listening to a word you're saying because your man's out there skittling them.'

'I've left Gillian to get a sandwich for her and Susan. I just hope they're not playing up. I mean, this is why I never go anywhere or do anything. They really saddle you, kids. But then you've never had that, have you? Have you got kiddies, Beverley?'

'He looks young to be a Metal Box Retired.'

'That's the Grunter.'

'Is it? Oh yes. He looks different with a hat on. Still looks young to be retired. Go on, Ron. Wipe the floor with him.'

A milder delivery, child of wayward thoughts about roast beef and Yorkshire pudding.

Then, the ball from hell . . .

ebbi, avesti, ebbe, avemmo, *Jack*, aveste, *Jack, Jack, Jack* . . .

exploding from its second bounce and finding its diabolical mark on a scantily guarded batsman. The Grunter, silenced, foetal, rolling into his agony with a thin white line of pain around his lips.

'Intimidation!'

'Intimidation be buggered.'

'Send him off.'

'What's happening, Jean?'

'Ron's hit the Grunter down below.'

142

'Is he all right?'

'Don't know. He's still rolling around.'

'Milking it a bit if you ask me.'

'Get on with it.'

'What's going to happen now?'

'Don't know. Vic'll probably give him a warning. They've got nearly ten minutes till Stumps.'

Umpire Shires, fighting laughter.

'Mr Glover. I'm giving you a warning about intimidatory bowling.'

'Sorry. I never meant it.'

'Right. So long as it doesn't happen again.'

'It won't.'

'Mr . . . what's his name?'

'Lubbock. He says he's in a lot of pain.'

'Mr Lubbock? Are you ready to resume?'

'I am not. The man's an animal. I've got a bruised testicle needs seeing to and as far as I'm concerned the match is scratched. Ungentlemanly behaviour.'

'That's up to your captain.'

'Well the captain's my brother and he'll agree with me.'

'I shall have to check with him. Shall we say a draw? And everybody into the Frank Whittle for a pint?'

'Is it buggery a draw. We've took six of their wickets. Oh please yourself. Who bloody cares. This is going to swell up like a balloon.'

Dog & Gun Sunday XI versus Metal Box Contemptibles, match abandoned, Lubbock, J. retired, hit upon the person.

'Tell you what, Glover, there's never a quiet moment when you're around, is there?'

'I never meant any harm.'

'That's no way for a bowler to talk.'

'But I didn't mean any harm.'

'No, I know that, you soft bastard. Anyway, don't worry about Lubbock. It wasn't as bad as he was making out.'

'Well played, chap.'

'Well played, Ronnie. Will you give us some coaching?'

'Thanks, Pearcie. How's the ankle?'

'Better than Lubbock's goolies.'

'Ron?'

'Eileen? Enjoying yourself?'

'Look at your trousers. I shall have to soak them. Are we getting a ride back with Vic and Jean?'

'Yeah, but not yet.'

'Well when?'

'After we've been for a drink. A few drinks.'

'You're not going to get silly?'

'I might.'

'I don't want you to get silly. And the girls are on their own, don't forget.'

'Eileen, put a sock in it. You wanted to come. I told you you wouldn't like it, but you would come, so now you're here just put a sock in it and fit in with what everybody else is doing, right?'

'Oi, Glover, what have you got in that bag?'

'Markham says they're Kent cobs.'

'Vic says they're Lubbock's nuts.'

'No, they're round the Frank Whittle being packed in ice.'

Funny old day. Funny how the bowling comes back. And the Italian. You think you're getting nowhere, but it's all in there, waiting to come out. You're doing all right, boy. For a thick house painter you're doing great. 'Thanks, Vic. I'll have a pint of mild and Eileen'll have a Snowball.'

'You've got a dog.'

'Eh?'

'He's watching you from the window. He looks heartbroken. Ah, look at him. Bring him with you.'

'Naah.'

'Go on. We don't mind, do we, Vic? We'd love a dog, only we're both out all day. Go on. Go and fetch him. He can go in the back with you.'

'You don't want him in your motor. He needs a bath and he farts like a trooper.'

' 'Course we want him. A walk's always better with a dog. What's his name?'

'Gums. Are you going to fetch him, Eileen, or am I?'

'I don't know where his lead is.'

'Don't you take him for walks as a rule then?'

'He takes himself. We just let him out and he comes back when he's done his business.'

'Well where's it likely to be? You'll have to come and help me look, Eileen.'

'I don't know where to look any more than you do. Try the sideboard. Why are men such babies, eh Jean?'

'Why don't we all come in and look for it, instead of sitting here talking about it? Eh Vic?'

'Yeah. Suits me, pet.'

'Yeah, we'll all come in and tell Gums he's coming for a run out to Bradgate Park. That's what you have to do with a dog, Ron. Tell him to fetch his own lead.'

'Or we could just take him without a lead. He'd be all right.'

'No. You don't know him, Vic. He'd run off and get lost. Either that or he'll start shagging some old lady's leg.'

'Ron!'

'Come on. While we're stood here arguing, we could have been in there, got his lead and gone.'

Eileen and Ronnie, Vic and Jean, in need of a lead, milling into the tiny kitchen with a very excited dog around their ankles.

'Back of the door?'

'No.'

'Kitchen cabinet?'

'No.'

'Sideboard?'

'Worth a try.'

'Don't let them see in there, Ron. I keep meaning to have a good clear-out. Tell you what, you sit down and I'll look.'

Ron, Vic and Jean, remaining standing, caught between curiosity and embarrassment.

'Nice little place you've got here. Eh Jean?'

'Mmm. I love your mirror. That's really nice. Gums. Go and find your lead there's a good boy. Go on. Then your Aunty Jean'll take you for a walk.'

'It was a wedding present, that mirror, wasn't it, Ron?'

'I don't know.'

'Yes, it was. He's never liked it. We didn't get much because people couldn't get stuff, but we did get that. I'll go and look upstairs.'

'No, we didn't get a lot neither. Not like they have wedding lists these days. It's our silver anniversary coming up, you know? In February. Twenty-five years. We're going to have a do at the Royal, a little dinner-dance.'

'Haven't you got a length of rope, Glover, down in that shed? A bit of string or something? Don't have to be a proper lead.'

'Might have.'

Ronnie, saturated with the shame and misery of having his sideboard opened in front of friends and the crappy utility mirror over his chimney breast being admired by a woman who's got an onyx table lamp, and his scabby dog not sitting when he's told to.

'You've got another visitor.'

'Eh?'

'Lady coming up your path in a camel coat.'

'Jehovah's Witness.'

'No. They always come in pairs. Eileen's gone to the door.'

'Who is it?'

'Can't hear.'

'Ron? Madame's here. From Susan's dancing.'

Those plans to chuck everything, start over, create a stylish and elegant living space. Too late. Madame has seen the nasty mirror. Vic and Jean, nodding and smiling like fools and not saying anything in case she's foreign. Too many chairs. Too many doilies. Jack, dark and lovely Jack, with a purple scarf against her long white throat, dominating that faded, crowded room, with a gentle crease of laughter round her eyes. From Ron, to the pouffe, to Gums, with his muzzle jammed hard into her crotch, and back to Ron.

*   *   *

'I'm so sorry to disturb you on a Sunday, and you've got visitors too. I meant to send a message with Susan yesterday and then I forgot.'

'You're lucky you caught us in, isn't she, Ron? We're just going for a run out.'

'Well I mustn't hold you up then. I just wondered when you could come and have a look at my sitting-room. If you'd still like the job?'

'Oh yes. Any time really. I could come tomorrow. Or if you want to look at pattern books it'd have to be Tuesday. After I've knocked off. Or later on. Whatever suits.'

'All right. Well let's say Tuesday, with some wallpaper patterns, at about seven? And I think I'm probably going to want stripes, if that cuts down on the pattern books for you?'

'Right you are.' *Get the dog off her, you dickhead. No, leave it. She's used to dogs. Worse to draw attention to it. Don't call her Jack, whatever you do.*

'Anyway, I'm keeping you. It's a lovely afternoon for a walk. Where are you going?'

'Bradgate. Or Beacon Hill. Somewhere out that way.'

'Oh yes, it's pretty there, isn't it? I sometimes take my girls out there. Anyway Ron, thanks very much, and we'll see you on Tuesday evening.'

'Bye, Madame.'

'I'll go ahead of you, Madame, because the door sticks. Susan's that excited about the panto. She's on about it all the time.'

'Well we're all excited about it. She's a sweet girl, Susan . . . Works very hard at her dancing. Bye-bye now.'

'That was Madame.'

'Seems very nice.'

'I liked her coat.'

'Susan idolizes her.'

'Glover, when Eileen was rooting around in that sideboard drawer, did I see a tie in there?'

'Could have. Why?'
'Fetch it out and give it here.'

Gums Glover, heading the procession out to the car, attached by a Burton's paisley tie to his new best friend, Vic Shires.

'That'll cost a bit. The Royal's not cheap, is it?'

'Well no. But it's not every day you celebrate your twenty-fifth, and I mean, we haven't got any kiddies to spend it on, so we might as well please ourselves. And they have different menus. Different prices. So you could have the one with soup, chicken and fruit cocktail, and that actually works out quite reasonable. But we're having melon, choice of roast, gâteau and cheese and biscuits. And then afterwards there's dancing and spot prizes. I'm really looking forward to it. And we shall have a lot of the old gang there that we used to hang round with. We were at school together, me and Vic, you know? All the way through. And there'll be two of my bridesmaids there. I had three but Pearl died. Only forty-seven. She found a lump and six weeks later she was gone.'

'How terrible.'

'No age, is it? Forty-seven.'

'We never do anything on our anniversary, do we, Ron? It falls just after Ron's birthday and we never do anything. We ought to do something.'

*　　*　　*

Eileen, catching hold of Ron's arm, tugging for his attention, vying with the dog-training theories of Vic Shires, and the stronger claim still of his own dark thoughts.

Why did you have to be there, with your fat ankles, going on about Susan and the dog's lead and everything. If I didn't live with you my living-room wouldn't look like that. I wouldn't have doilies. I wouldn't be anything like I have to be now, if I didn't have you holding me back. Cluttering the place up.

'See, a dog is a pack animal. He'll follow whoever he thinks is boss.'

'I can tell you now who he thinks is boss. His dick.'

'No, no, no. Granted a dog will go out of his way to get his oats, but if his pack leader tells him to go in the opposite direction, he will.'

'Never.'

'See, Gums doesn't know who his leader is. If he thought you were the boss, he'd do what you said and it wouldn't matter how much rumpy he was missing out on. Mind, I think you have to start with them when they're still a pup.'

'Get away. Dick's king with Gums. He even does it with the roly-poly.'

'What?'

'The roly-poly Eileen puts down in the winter, to stop draughts under the door. He even has it off with that.' *Stop pulling on my arm, woman. I hate it.* 'Not a bad life though, Vic. As much grub and sleep and rumpy as you want. No electric bills to worry about.'

'And being able to lick your own balls.'

'Yep.'

151

'We ought to get a little car.'

'Well first I'd have to get a little driving licence and a big pile of money.'

'It wouldn't take that much. Not a little second-hand one. Vic and Jean seem to manage all right.'

'Eileen, you're like a long-playing record. Whatever Jean's got you think we've got to have, and it's only five minutes ago you didn't even want to go round there and meet her. And now it's Vic and Jean this and Vic and Jean that. It's different for them. They've not got two girls growing up, needing stuff all the time. And they had money when Jean's Dad died. Vic's a great mate and Jean's a very nice woman, but if I hear their names one more time today I shall do somebody an injury.'

'You've been nasty all afternoon.'

'No I haven't. Saying we're not having a wedding anniversary party's not being nasty.'

'How come other people can do these things but we have to be different?'

'How come other people have coffee you can smell and paintings of figs, and bookshelves? Eh? Bookshelves in the kitchen.'

'You're round the bend.'

'How come other people don't have *Titbits* lying around all over the place and a crinoline lady on the mantelpiece? Eh? How come other people have got room to swing a cat if anybody comes? How come other people aren't all crapped up with china cabinets and horrible chairs?'

'Other people do have *Titbits*. What are you doing?'

'What does it look like I'm doing?'

'Where are you going with it?'

'Down the garden.'

'Ron?'

'Don't try to stop me, Eileen. If I don't do this I shall do something worse.'

Ronnie Glover, in his Sunday shirt and his best trousers, running from the house, shouting, noise, no words, flying to his shed, hurling paint cans and deck-chairs out into the autumn evening, in his search for methylated spirit. People watching. Eileen, anxious, in the kitchen window. Gums, from a safe distance. Robbo, out in his garden, and somebody at an upstairs window of number 27. All watching his wild splashing with the bottle of meths, fumbling with matches, kicking at the pyre and cursing it and then punching the sky for joy as the flames take hold.

'Die, you ugly bastard. Die.'

Susan, arriving home from tea at Annette's.

'What's happening?'

'Oh nothing. Your Dad's just gone barmy. He's burning the pouffe.'

T uesday. Stew with carrots and boiled potatoes, plums and custard, and a pot of tea.

'I'm stuffed.'

'Dad, Mum, in France, right, they have their dinners different to ours. In France, they'd have stew, and then they'd have the carrots afterwards. And then the potatoes. Then they'd have some stinky cheese. And then pudding. We did it in French. Mademoiselle Riley says the French are very civilized at table, and she says they sit there for hours. She says they could still be sitting there at ten o'clock.'

'What for?'

'Talking. Eating.'

'What, and then have to get cleared up at that time of night?'

'Yeah.'

'I shouldn't like that. I like to get cleared up.'

'I wouldn't mind having my carrots separate.'

'Yes, well you would say that, wouldn't you. Anyway, before

you disappear down that shed I want you to have a look at the dog.'

'I'm not disappearing down the shed. Well I am, but not for long. I'm taking the wallpaper samples round to Madame's.'

'I know. But I still want you to have a look at the dog. He's been scratching himself all day.'

'What am I looking for?'

'Fleas.'

'What do they look like?'

'I don't know. You should know. You always reckoned you had them when you were at home.'

'We had the bites. But you never see them actually doing it. I know what bedbugs look like. They used to drop off the wall on to the mattress. Eileen, I can't do it. I've got to go out. Have you got anything to put on him? Any powder?'

'Yes.'

'Susan, do the dog, there's a good girl.'

'What time will you be back?'

'Don't know. I've got to measure up. Then they've got to choose the paper. And I shall probably stop for a drink. Tony likes to have a chat and a drink.'

'Annette's Mum says he's never there. She says they lead separate lives.'

'Well he is there, because I had a drink with him when I was doing the kitchen.'

'What is separate lives, Mum?'

'Ask your Dad.'

'Annette's Mum says they've got twin beds and they've got a daughter in South Africa who never writes.'

'Where's she got all that from?'

'Annette's aunty did their cleaning.'

'When?'

'Ages ago.'

'Couldn't have been ages ago. They've only been there about eighteen months.'

155

'That's when it was. Ages ago. About eighteen months.'

'And she's not old enough to have a daughter in South Africa.'

'Oh I don't know, Ron. I thought when I saw her close up on Sunday, "You're not as young as you make out." '

'How old do you have to be, Dad?'

'Susan, clear the plates and do the dog.'

Ronnie, raging with loyalty for Jack, on his way upstairs for a quick wash of the armpits, pausing briefly by the crinoline lady on the mantelpiece.

'You're next.'

'You poor baby. You look like a beast of burden. I should have fetched the pattern books myself. I forget about your not having a car.'

'No, that's all right. They're not that heavy. Just an awkward size. You were happy with the kitchen, then?'

'I love it. Love it to pieces. I'm not at home very much but when I am here I absolutely live in that kitchen, and now it's perfect. Sunshine whatever the weather. Come through, come through. Red or white?'

'Sorry?'

'Wine. Red or white?'

Red goes with beef. White goes with fish. 'Oh, whichever's opened.' *Wazzock.*

'Well, I've got white already opened, and red very easily opened because it's not like brain surgery, so how about we start with a glass of white and then move on?'

'Yeah, lovely.' *Two bottles. Bloody hell.* 'And what I can do, is, if your hubby's not around tonight, measure up, give you an idea how many rolls it'll take, and then leave you the books for a day or two, while you make your minds up.'

'Oh no, not at all.'

Jack, with her hair loose and her shoes slipped off, and her dark green dress buttoned tightly to the neck, patting the place beside her on the long, beige couch.

156

'No, Tony's in Singapore till next week so I'm going to make my decision tonight and get on with it. I can't bear hanging about.'

'It's a nice room.'

'It is. And quite wasted. We hardly ever sit in here. But still, it needs doing. I thought stripes. What do you think?'

'Yep. Stripes would be nice.'

'Are they tricky?'

'What, to match? No. Stripes are easy. You'll need a lot though. It's a big room.'

'All right. Well all of that's your department. Cheers, anyway.'

A cold, fruity sizzle on a palate still beset by stew and plums.

'Cheers.' *A bit sour. Nice though. Very nice.* 'There's a lot of stripes in this book.'

'I thought blue, or grey, or even pink, as long as it's not a really pinky pink. Have you always been a painter and decorator, Ron?'

'Just about. Since I came out of the Navy.'

'How long were you in the Navy?'

'Four years. When I came out my Dad said to get into the building trade. He said I'd never be out of work. I was never any good with wood, and I didn't fancy brickying, so I went in for painting.'

'And you enjoy it?'

' 'S all right. Plumbing would have been better. Licence to print money. But painting's all right. You get to make things look nice.'

'You certainly do. I think it's a lovely way to earn a living.'

'Have you always been in dancing?'

'Always. Since I was three. I got too tall for ballet so I did variety chorus, and then I got married and did quite a lot of ballroom, and we moved around, all over the place, and I've ended up teaching in most of the places we've lived.'

'Where were you before you moved here?'

'That's a nice one. Green. I hadn't considered green. What do you think?'

'Yes. Nice. With your settees and stuff all being beige, you could have anything really.'

There speaks a man who's got every shade of shite in his house and a living-room like the black hole of Calcutta.

'More white? Or shall we start on the red?'

'Whatever you like.' *You're getting the come-on. No. Yes you are.* 'How's the panto going?'

'Organized chaos. But you're going to help us. I haven't forgotten. There's a man from the Am Drams called Barry or Terry or something, and he's in charge of the scenery. He needs all the help he can get, so I'll give him your number.'

Tell her. She knows already. She just forgets. 'We're not on the phone.'

'Oh no, of course. Why is that?'

'Don't know. Just never got round to it.'

'You should have a telephone. Then people could call you and ask you to do decorating. You could advertise. You need a telephone if you're in business.'

Look at that little bit that dips in between her collar bones. Dips in, soft as a baby's bum. She's never got a daughter in South Africa. 'Do you ever teach ballroom?'

'I have done. Not many people want it these days, but I used to do a lot. Want some lessons?'

'Well . . . It's just this thing we're supposed to be going to. A silver wedding. A dinner-dance. Not till after Christmas. Ages yet. But we've never really done any dancing.'

'I'll teach you. Bring your wife and I'll teach you.'

Fuck. 'Perhaps we could. I don't know. Eileen's always so busy.'

'I'll teach you then. I'll teach you and then you can teach her.'

Go for it, Glover. 'Yeah. That'd be really nice.'

'I like this green. I think I'm going for that one.'

'You ought to sleep on it. It's a big decision.'

'I will sleep on it. Let me top you up. So what rank did you get to in the Navy? Mind your feet a minute.'

*   *   *

Jack, rolling back the rug, moving a little table, bending, lifting, with big, smooth movements, leaning over the back of another settee into a box of records, sticking her rear out like a cat on heat.

'Oh I was only a Petty Officer.' *What the fuck's she doing?*

'Come on then. On your feet. I'll show you the foxtrot. Do you know how to hold me? Yes. But bring this hand a little higher, and relax it. My back's not going to bite you. That's it. And this hand, just palm to palm. No need to squeeze it. Now this is going to help you steer me, because you're going to be in charge. Hm? So the best thing is to be relaxed but firm. Lovely. I'll just put some music on. And what we're going to do is . . .'

Jesus . . .

'. . . we're just going to walk to the rhythm. All right? We're not going to worry about steps. Just listen to the music, feel the rhythm, and walk it through.'

'You'll have to tell me when to start.'

'I will. For the first few times. Stop worrying. Listen to a few bars and shift your weight onto your right foot, so when we start you'll step forward with your left foot first.'

'Left foot first.'

Ronnie, breaking sweat, feeling his sensitive artist's fingers turn to pork sausages, and the warmth of Jack's belly invading his slacks. *Hear the rhythm. Hear the fucking rhythm. Left foot first. When she says.*

'And, left, right, off we go. Just walk.'

'Sorry.'

'That's OK. Start again. Just walk. You're trying to make it harder than it is. Walk, but relax into it. Exaggerate it a bit. Play around with it. Nobody's watching. Yes. *Yes!* That's it. Now why did you do that?'

'What did I do?'

'As soon as I told you you'd got it, you stuck your bum out.

159

Look at us. All of a sudden you could build a housing estate between us. How can you lead me if I can't feel you?'

'Sorry.'

'Never mind sorry. Come back and we'll start again. And again, left, right, yes. That's nice. Keep going.'

Jack Granger, on her third drink of the evening, enjoying the rare, clumsy innocence of a man who doesn't know he's attractive. Grazing his cheek with her lips, nuzzling his ear.

'You're very good. Very natural. I think you're ready for some steps.'

God, don't let there be a little damp patch on my trousers. Have a look. Are you mad? Don't look. Don't ever look.

'Now this is simple. Left forward, brush right, step to the side with your left, and close right to left. Now backwards, left, brush right, left to the side, close right to left. And forwards again. Left, brush right, yes, yes. Can you see how you're dancing in a zig-zag? Keep going. Keep the rhythm. Lovely. Wonderful. You're a very fast learner. Now do it with me. Hands. Remember, I don't bite.'

Ah God, the smell of her. Where her hair lifts away from her scalp. Like vinegar, but not. She must be nearly six foot. If she was shorter I'd be in real trouble. Left forward, brush right, side left, close right. Think of ice cubes. Think of Eileen. And Tony. She's got a daughter in South Africa. I'm tangled in my Y-fronts. If I could just ease the old feller up the way. Just ease him round. Think of wallpaper. How many rolls? Twenty? Twenty-two? Christ I could shag the arse off her and then die happy.

'Don't force it. And stop planning ahead all the wrong moves. If you must think ahead, plan on doing it perfectly. I can see you, steeling yourself for a big mistake. It's a bad attitude to life Ron. Hm? Prepared for the worst. *That's* it. You're leading and you don't even know it. Wonderful. See? When you shift your weight I feel I have to shift mine because you're moving your whole body. People think you dance with just your feet, but you don't. Don't

160

stop breathing. Now tighter. Closer into me, and shorter steps. If you're going to a dinner-dance you might only have a postage stamp to dance on. Shorter steps. Yes. See? Even if I'd never danced with you before I'd be able to dance with you because you're leading me now. See?'

'Yeah.'

Ronnie, smiling, so proud he could bust, and a dick like a telegraph pole jammed down the leg of his trousers.

'No, don't slump. I know you're getting tired, but you'll get stronger. Yes. You're making me feel what you want. Can you feel what I want, Ron?'

Jesus. This isn't happening. This is one of your Mary Tyler Moore dreams and Jack got mixed up in it because of the big beige sofa and her long dancer's legs. Ah Jesus. This'll never happen to you again, ever. This is your one go in paradise, Glover. Say something. You pillock, say something. 'What do I do when we get to a corner?' *I didn't say that. You did.*

'Ssh. Corners are lesson two. I think we've gone nearly as far as we need to today. Stand still. Keep the rhythm, without the steps, and stay close.'

She can't be doing what it feels like she's doing. She is. Ah no. I never washed down there. Why didn't I? Go to the bog now and do it quick. Are you crazy? You've blown it. A beautiful woman is rummaging down the front of your trews and you've got a knob that smells like Danish Blue. You don't deserve anything in life, Glover. You always balls things up.

'Here. Against the wall. I love it with my clothes on against the wall.'

Say something. 'You're beautiful, Jack.' *Touch her somewhere. Kiss her and touch her. Tits first.* 'You're beautiful, Jack.'

'Pull my skirt up. I'm in a hurry.'

Straight in, boy. She's red hot. Straight in. Oh fuck. Please God, not that. Anything. Anything. But please don't do this to me.

*   *   *

161

Ronnie, insinuated in folds of dark green wool and the desperate bucking of Jack's pelvis, positioning himself for penetration with a telegraph pole that has shrunk to the size of an acorn.

'Sorry.'

'Doesn't matter, doesn't matter. I love it soft. Push it in with your thumb. It'll get harder when I squeeze it. Quick. Quick. For Chrissakes, Ron, don't stop.'

Ronnie Glover, cycling home with wallpaper pattern books and an erection for which he no longer has any use, pausing to look at his reflection in the Co-op window to see whether he looks like a man who has just had sex.

What a woman. What a handful. Jesus. So bloody cool. Choosing wallpaper one minute and then screaming she wants her knickers off. She'd have had anybody. No she wouldn't. She said you were sweet. Yeah, but. She did. She said you were sweet and when the old feller let you down she went wild. Hope Eileen's having an early night. I'd like to sit in the dark and just think about it. Remember it all. Eileen might smell it. No. Sex does smell. Yeah but Eileen might not know that. And you only smell it if you're sniffing for it. Have a bath anyway. Be on the safe side. Think up a reason why you'd have a bath on a Tuesday.'

'You took your time.'

'She kept changing her mind, and she wanted to decide tonight so I can get it ordered. What are you doing?'

'Twink Home Perm.'

'How long does it take?'

'Another hour. Why?'

'I thought I'd have a bath.'

'It's Tuesday.'

'Yeah. I've got backache.'

'I'm not surprised, humping those pattern books around. She could have gone to the showroom and sorted it herself. She's got a car.'

'Yeah, well . . .'

'Are you all right?'

'Yeah. Just tired. Are you all right?'

'Shall be if this Twink's worked.'

'Is there any water?'

'Should be.'

'I'll go on up then. Have a bit of a soak.'

'Stop up there. Have an early night. You look all in.'

'Yeah, I think I will.'

'Shall I bring you a cup of tea?'

'No, you're all right.'

'Slice of ginger cake?'

'No thanks.' *Stop being so bloody nice. I've just fucked another woman and she's being dead nice and offering me cake. What if she offers me sex? Eileen never offers sex. Still. Please don't let her find out. Please, not ever. And please let it happen again with Jack, now I know, not caught by surprise. Please let me remember it all. Every bit that happened. Especially the bit when she said Yes and she was away, somewhere lovely, you could tell from her eyes.*

'Was that Yes to cake or Yes to tea? Hello? Anybody home?'

'Did you see *Z Cars* last night?'

'No mate, I didn't.'

'Fancy Smith had a set-to with the desk sergeant.'

'Yeah?'

'I think he was in the right, but Jock Weir wouldn't back him up, so he's got suspended. I'm not watching it next week. Not if he's suspended.'

'He'll be back in it next week.'

'No. Suspended till his disciplinary hearing.'

'It's only a telly programme, lad. He's not really suspended.'

'I *know* that. Our Diane's going to write in.'

'Pearcie?'

'Yeah?'

'What do they call you at home?'

'How do you mean?'

'Well, like here, we all call you Pearce, or Pearcie, don't we?'

'Yeah?'

'Or Fierce Pearce, sometimes.'

164

'Yeah?'

'So what does your Mam call you?'

'Raymond.'

'Is that right? Raymond. Oi, Shires, it's twenty to ten. Who's mashing this morning?'

'I am. I'm just going.'

'Good. I'm parched. Here, do you know Pearcie's real name?'

'Yes.'

'What then?'

'Can't just remember. I do know it. Is it Douglas?'

'No.'

'It's something like Douglas.'

'No it isn't.'

'Give us your cans then. I'm going to try that big party in Plot 86.'

'What did you watch last night, Ron?'

'Nothing. I was out. I had a job to price for a lady I know.' *A lady who snaked her dancer's legs around me.* 'And then I had a bath and an early night.'

'What job are you going to do for her?'

'Papering her living-room.'

'I could help you if you like.'

'No, you're all right, lad. I'm better working on my own.' *Working on my own with slow masterful strokes, heedless of everything but her wild, animal cries. Jesus fucking Christ, why couldn't you have managed a bit of that last night? . . .*

A flutter in the belly, and Ronnie's slightly bruised cock twitching in agreement, pressed against a rung of the ladder.

'. . . Tell you what though, Pearce. You can give me a hand when we knock through at home.'

'Great. Shall I come tonight?'

'No, you pillock. I don't know when it'll be. Sometime. Big job, knocking through. A lot of banging and dust. And then making good. Plastering.'

165

'Norrie could come and do your plastering.'

'No need for that. We can manage without Chater. Wiring. Might have to get somebody for the wiring. But the decorating. You can help me with that. Have a few beers maybe. But I don't know when.'

'Tea's up. And I've remembered. It's Raymond.'

'Vic's remembered it.'

'It just came to me. I knew it was something like Douglas.'

Vic Shires, Ronnie Glover and Raymond Pearce, breaking for tea after an hour and a half on exterior doors and windows, Fletcher's Common Estate, Phase Three.

'How was Plot 86?'

'Told me to piss off.'

'Who brewed up for you then?'

'She did. I asked her if she missed being in show business.'

'Yer what?'

'I said, "I've got all of your records at home." '

'Yeah?'

'So she put the kettle on.'

'Yeah?'

'And I said, "I told the wife last night, Ruby Murray's moved into Plot 86. Either that else it's her kid sister." '

'Yeah?'

'I said, "Sing us a bit of 'Softly, softly'." '

'Yeah?'

'Then the kettle boiled. And she says, "Are you coming back for a shag at dinner time, or what?" '

*C*ould go to a different one. Could go to the one in The Parade,
only Markham might see me. Or just go to the usual place and buy
extra. How many? There's a packet not opened yet, indoors, so
that's three weeks' worth for Eileen, four weeks if she gets her
whassisname. So get another packet to use with Jack and keep them
separate. One packet enough? How would you know? Go to the
usual place, get three packets, keep two of them down the shed.
Yeah.

Ronnie Glover, arriving home with three packets of Durex, a tin
of Eucryl Tooth Powder he picked up to look casual while he was
asking for the Durex, and a bottle of brilliantine he really did
mean to buy. Thursday. Toad-in-the-hole, baked beans and mash.
Green jelly with banana in it.

'Have you been round Madame's?'
    'No. Why?' *Act natural.*
    'You're late.'

'Oh yeah. No, I saw Markham. Stopped for a chat.'

'Well get washed before this dries out any more. We've had ours.'

'I'll dish it out if you like, Eileen, if you want to watch your programme.'

'No, I'll do it. I've got to talk to you about something.'

She knows. She can't do.

'Shall I make a fresh pot?'

'Later. I'll have my dinner first.' *Look at her face. You'll tell by her face if she knows. No. She doesn't know.* 'What's up?'

'Ma and Pop. I went round this afternoon.'

'Yeah?'

'Pop. It's got to be said, Ron. I think he's going peculiar.'

'He's always been peculiar.' *No he hasn't.*

'No he hasn't. I think he's going senile. I mean, one minute he's sitting gazing out of the window with a silly grin on his face. He doesn't hear anything you say to him. And then he turns, all of a sudden, and he's that nasty. He called Ma a niggling old bat and she'd hardly said anything to him.'

'Did he?' *She definitely doesn't know. In the clear, Glover.*

'And he's not sleeping. Ma says he's up half the night, shuffling about and she reckons, now I don't know if this is true, but she reckons he's gone wandering off a couple of times. In the middle of the night.'

'He's all right.'

'No he's not. Allow me to know about these things. He's not eating. Ma opened a tin of macaroni cheese for their dinner and he wouldn't touch it. And I could smell drink on him.'

'Does he look ill?'

'No, but that's not the point, is it?'

'I don't know.'

'The point is, Ron, if he's wandering in his mind, what's going to happen to them? The point is, we can't have them here.'

'They're all right where they are.'

'Well I don't think they are all right. How would you like it if

168

somebody called you a niggling old bat for nothing and you had to chuck their macaroni cheese away? It's wearing Ma down. You can see it.'

'So what are you saying?'

'I'm saying he needs watching. You're going to have to go round there more and keep an eye. Because if he is starting to wander, we shall have to, you know . . .'

'What?'

'See about something.'

'What?'

'A home or something.'

'Get away. I shall be in a home before he is.'

'Well don't say I haven't warned you.'

'No. All right. But he's always called her a niggling old bat. He just used to do it under his breath. And she is a niggling old bat, Eileen, let's face it. She's a horrible woman. And I'll tell you what. I'd sooner he was having a few drinks and going out for a shuffle without getting written bloody permission, than sitting in front of that sodding telly all the time. I mean, it's only five minutes ago you were complaining he was getting too wrapped up in the telly and not getting to the lav in time. If he's stopped dribbling in his trousers and he's getting out more, that's got to be an improvement.'

'It's not an improvement. It's a change. Anyway. I'm just saying. That's all.'

'Yeah. All right. I tell you what I did wonder. Should we see about getting the telephone put in?'

'Ooh yes.'

'Then if anything was to crop up, it'd be easier for them to get us round there fast.'

'Ooh yes.'

'And it'd be handy for me as well. You know? For people wanting their decorating doing. They could phone up.'

'Ooh yes. Can we manage it, do you think?'

'Won't know till we try, will we?'

'Ooh Ron. I've always wanted to be on the telephone. Will we be in the book?'

'Yeah. Sure to be.'

' 'Course. Ma and Pop won't be on the phone, so that wouldn't really make any difference.'

'No. But the Duchess is on the phone.'

'Oh yes.'

'So, any problems, Ma could go round next door and get on the blower to us.'

'Yes. Oh it's going to be lovely. Wait till I tell them at work. And I shall be able to phone Jean.'

'Yep. Just so long as you've not got any long lost cousins in Australia you've never told me about.'

'Eat your sausages before they go cold. Ooh, come here and let me give you a kiss. You're not such a bad old stick, are you? Sometimes.'

Eileen Glover, in a peach twinset and a failed home perm, embracing her husband from behind, aroused by the promise of going up in the world. Ronnie, repelled by the embrace he so recently longed for, doing battle with overcooked Yorkshire pudding, concerned to find a hiding place for two packets of extra-mural johnnies, cradling his happy, sinful secret.

'Ron?'

'Yeah?'

'We shall have to get a little table to stand it on in the hall.'

S lip *home at dinner time. If asked, say, need to collect paper-*
trimmer. No. Say, need to pick up some money. Or a prescription.
Yeah. Go home, get change of socks, wash armpits, collect whassis-
names from shed, ride back to site without getting sweaty. No
problem.

'Where are you off?'
  'I've got to nip home.'
  'How come?'
  'Dog's not well.'
  'What's up with him?'
  'Off his food. And his nose is hot.'
  'I'll run you.'
  'No, no. You're all right.'
  'I'll run you, you silly bastard. You're going to be creased biking
it there and back in an hour.'
  Well done, Glover. You've handled that well. 'Thing is, Vic, I've
got a couple of other little things to do as well, while I'm there.'

'That's all right. It'll make a change.'

'What about your snap?'

'I'll bring it with me. Eat it there. Pearcie, I'm running Glover home for half an hour because his dog's a bit middling. Do you want to come?'

'Yeah.'

Ronnie Glover, formerly on a top-secret mission to enter his house, prepare his body for sex and leave again, undetected, now accompanied by men with packed lunches. Men moved by concern for a lonely, ailing dog.

'Oops. I think he's feeling better, Glover.'

Cheers, you bastard hound. Why don't you run the three-minute mile and make a complete fucking liar of me? 'He's a lot brighter than he was this morning.'

'He's all right, aren't you, my son? His nose is a bit hot but he's probably had it stuck up his bum all morning. Any chance of a brew?'

'Yeah. Anyone for a bacon sandwich?'

Ronnie, made reckless by the massive irregularity of bringing people home in the middle of a working day and allowing them to drop crumbs. Vic, laying bacon rashers in a pan and sliced bread on the cabinet top. Pearce, making tea, properly, warming the pot, counting out the spoons. Gums, the miraculously revived invalid, seeing off cheese rolls, luncheon meat sandwiches, and a Co-op pasty, without anything touching the sides.

'I shan't be a mo. Just got something to do.' *Think, Glover, think. Bathroom first. Shave? Not enough time. Wash armpits, feet and the old feller. Get a clean pair of socks and put them in your pocket for later. Change Y-fronts. Can't. Eileen'll notice. There is no way you're going to be able to get a clean pair of kecks off that pile without Eileen picking it up on her radar. Go on. You've had all that bacon so you're dead anyway. What a sod's opera. It's my airing cupboard and they're my kecks and I helped beat Hitler, Mussolini and the fucking Japs, and if I want to slip home one dinner time to freshen up, I can do. Yeah. Even if you are doing it to make sure your tackle's clean and nice for another woman, you cheating lying bastard.*

Ronnie, arguing with himself in front of Eileen's precision-folded laundry, too flustered with guilt and excitement to question why Gillian's duffle-bag was dumped on the landing, and the toilet seat was up. Too conflicted between the desire to seem nonchalant and the need to wash the frying-pan to remember about the Durex he has hidden in a pile of old *Picture Posts* in the shed.

'What are you doing?'

'Taking the scenic route.'

Oh my God. She's doing it.

'All right up there?'

'Yup.'

'Just yup?'

'I'm having to . . . Can you just stop a minute? I'm having to . . .
you know . . . else I shan't last. I shall just boil over.'

'I shan't let you.'

'No?'

'You can tell when a man's getting close.'

'Can you?'

'Yes. Your balls change just before you come. Why don't men
ever know that?'

Oh my God. She's studying my balls.

'So then I stop. Let you calm down a bit. Then I start again.'

'Yeah?'

'And that's how I carry on. Stopping and starting. So when I do let you come, you think you've died and gone to heaven. You do like it this way?'

'Yeah.' *Oh God, yeah. This is what some men get. Some men get this at home. Jeee-sus. Ah, that's sweet. She's found that little bit of skin. Better stop soon, Jack.* Voglio, vuoi, vuole, VUOLE, *she can't be watching my balls*, vuole vogliamo, vogliamo, *OH MY GOD*.

'Sorry.'

'Never mind Sorry. Was it nice?'

'Ah God.'

'Is that as in Ah God, Yes?'

'Lovely. Best ever.'

'Steady on.'

'It was. I mean it. My old feller's got a smile on his face.'

'You're right. He has. Well I'm glad it was good. I could have stopped you, but I didn't want to. I wanted to see you come all unravelled, all to pieces. That's the second-best bit of it for me.'

'Yeah?' *Jesus, now where's she going?*

'Yeah. Now it's my turn for the best bit.'

'We might have a bit of a wait. You know? He doesn't bounce back the way he used to. Old age.' *Christ Almighty.*

'No. I don't want him hard. I want him like this.'

Jack Granger, blue crêpe bunched around her waist with one arm, kneeling astride him, rocking against him, small, but plump enough still, wet enough, gently, then sharper, letting her skirt fall but catching it up again so she can still see her own long legs. Jack, with a flushed throat and the threat of cramp in her thigh, rearing above him, never breaking rhythm, shuddering to a dry, desperate sob. And Ronnie, melting. Gathering her down onto his chest, stroking her hair.

'I've got to get washed and changed.'

'What?'

'I need a quick shower. I'm late.'

'What for?'

'I've got to go and talk to the Am Drams about the pantomime. Anyway, you need to get on.'

'Yeah. Jack?'

'Mm.'

'That was lovely.'

'Good. Fuck, I've got cramp.'

'I'll rub it for you.'

'No. Walking on it's the best thing. Time I wasn't here.'

'Yeah.'

Furniture to move. Dustsheets to spread. Walls to strip. Ronnie Glover, down behind a sofa, half out of his boiler suit. Abandoned. With the kind of ache in his throat that big boys get when they don't cry.

She could have stayed for a bit of a cuddle. That's what women like, isn't it? A nice cuddle without the old pecker prodding up against them. A box of choccies. Card on their anniversary. Not straight down, gobble, gobble, and then gone to talk about the panto. Dunno though. There was that Wren. But that was wartime. Women were different then. Still. Keeping all her clobber on. What's that all about? Two shags and I've still not seen her arse.

'Wall lights.'

'Yeah?'

'I shall have to decorate again afterwards, but it'll be worth it.'

'Right.'

'We've seen them in this new showroom. All sorts. The ones we're having, they've got wooden brackets, carved, like little scrolly shapes, and they have these little pointed bulbs and then a little shade on top. Jean'll probably make the shades. She's handy like that. They're the latest thing in lighting, anyway.'

'Yeah?'

'You all right, Glover?'

'Yeah.'

'My best pal all right?'

'What?'

'Gums.'

'Oh. Yeah.'

'You look all in.'

'I am. I've got this job on. Papering a lounge in Gartree Road.'

'Want a hand?'

'No, no. And I've got Eileen on, wanting stuff done at home, and I've been volunteered for painting scenery for this panto Susan's in. I never get a minute.'

'Where's the panto?'

'St Columba's.'

'Here, Pearce, this might be up your street. Painting scenery for the panto.'

'Yeah. When do we start?'

'Next week. Only I don't know how many they want. I haven't actually talked to the bloke myself. It's just Jack volunteered me.'

'Who's Jack?'

'Madame. Susan's dancing teacher. It's her lounge I'm papering.'

'Jack?'

'Yeah. It's short for Jacqueline.'

'Ah, you mean Jackie. Jackie's short for Jacqueline. The one in the camel coat the other Sunday?'

'Yes.'

'Very nice. Jackie. Well, no wonder you're looking like an old rag.'

'What do you mean?'

'Nothing. What I say. If you're putting in a full day here and then doing a job at night, no wonder you're beat. You want to ease off a bit.'

'I'm all right.'

' 'Course you are.' *No you're not, Glover.* 'What you want to do is, have five minutes in the chair after tea. I always do. Five minutes shut-eye, then I'm set up. Fit for anything. All right, young Pearce? St Columba's, next . . . when was it?'

'Don't know yet.'

'Yeah well. St Columba's, whenever Glover tells you. You *shall* go to the ball, Raymond.'

Vic Shires doing a very good fairy godmother, in a pair of bib and brace overalls.

F riday. Chips and egg and lemon curd tard.

'Hi, Dad. Gillian's in trouble.'
  'Is she?'
  'Mum's upstairs shouting at her and I'm keeping an eye on the chip pan.'
  'Good. What's it about?'
  'Something about knickers.'
  'Right.'

'Eileen?'
  'I've had it with her, Ron. I've absolutely had it with her. She's a little slapper and we might as well chuck her out on the street now because that's where she's going to end up.'
  'What's happened?'
  'She never went to school today.'
  'Susan, be quiet and spread some bread.'
  'So she's been bunking off?'

'Bunking off's only the start of it. She was here yesterday as well because there was a load of bacon missing, only she says she didn't have it. So I came back early today. To check up on her. I swapped with Lilian, so I shall have to go in early to do veg on Monday. Get back here and what do I find? Madam's upstairs, half-naked with a van driver from Wildt Mellor Bromley.'

'What, *my* Madame?'

'Don't be stupid. Not Madame. Madam. Gillian. Susan, watch those chips and stop ear-holing.'

'So what happened?'

'It's what'd already happened I'm more worried about.'

'Do you think they'd?'

'Well her knickers were on the landing, so what do you think?'

'And what did he say?'

'Nothing. I let fly at her and by the time I turned round to start on him, he'd scarpered.'

'And what does she say?'

'She says it's boring at school and she's going to get a flat with what'shisname.'

'Scott.'

'What?'

'He's called Scott. He's twenty-five and Gillian's done it with him.'

'Put the kettle on and stop interrupting. God alone knows what she's been up to with him.'

'Well, Eileen, I think we all know what she's been up to. Question is, what do we do now?'

'I've had enough, Ron. I've had nothing but cheek and answering back for months, and now this. She's disgusting. I don't know where she ever gets these ideas from. I'm warning you, Ron. I'm right on the edge. I have it all to do. Shopping. Cleaning. Cooking. You're never here. We used to be a nice little family, and the girls were nice. When they used to have their matching little dresses. And you weren't down that shed all the time, drawing pictures.

181

Reading books. We were all right then. And now it's all gone wrong. She doesn't care, you know? She's sat up there in her room and she couldn't care less. I'm the one who's upset. It's no wonder my home perm didn't take.'

'I'll help you, Mum. Shall I do the eggs?'

'I'm not hungry.'

'I am. Should I go up and see her?'

'Have your tea first. Susan'll do your eggs. I couldn't face a thing.'

Lights on, curtains closed. The year has turned. Ronnie and Susan, cosy in the battle's lull, tackling egg and chips for four.

'And I know she had that bacon because the wrapper was in the bin, and anyway, I could smell it.'

'Leave it, Eileen. Missing bacon's the least of our worries.' *Own up, you slippery bastard.* 'I'll go up and have a word.'

Gillian. A stranger. Just a blotchy little pudding with bitten nails and arms running to fat. And thick. Too thick even to pass College of Preceptors Typing.

How could I have a kid this thick? Susan'll go to college. Susan's my girl. Don't think that. But I do think that. 'Gillian?'

'What?'

'Your Mum's been telling me.'

'Cow.'

'Now don't start.'

'No, don't *you* start. I never had that bacon.'

'Ah. The bacon doesn't matter. It's not the bacon we're talking about.'

'I am.'

'We're worried about you, Gill.' *Gillian. You never call her Gill.* 'You should be in school, getting your exams. There's plenty of time for boys and that later on. I mean, what if you fell for a baby? It could happen, you know?'

182

'I hope you're not going to give me a talk.'

'Bit late for that, by the sounds of things. But you're not old enough. You do realize that? Does he know how old you are?'

'Yeah.'

'Well then, he knows he could get into a lot of trouble.'

'I'm nearly sixteen.'

'You're fifteen and a half. Anyway, that's not the point.'

'What is the point?'

Good question. 'You should be in school.'

'What were you doing here yesterday anyway, not telling Mum? I heard you. Fiddling around in the airing cupboard. What were you up to?'

She could hold this over you for evermore. Come clean. Tell Eileen you were here and you had the bacon. Make something up. Anything. Shit, no. 'Never mind that. What I do in my house is my business, and before you start opening your big mouth to your Mum, remember, we've got an anniversary coming up. Eh? Secrets? Surprises?'

'You haven't got no secrets and surprises. I had a look after you'd gone. What? What secret is it?'

'Wouldn't be a secret if I told you.'

'Well if it's a secret, why did you bring Nob-Head and Dick-Face home with you?'

'This is all completely off the point, Gillian. So here's the bad news. You're going to school tomorrow . . . '

'Tomorrow's Saturday.'

'You're going to school Monday. You're staying at school and we're going to keep checking up on you. And this lad is banned. If he's twenty-five he's old enough to know better. So he's banned.'

'You can't do that. Anyway, we're going to get engaged.'

'Fine. You get engaged. Get engaged, get married, move out, piss off, and then you won't be my problem any more.' *Oh yes she will.*

'I hate this house.'

'You and me both. Now straighten up and fly right, or clear off and bugger your life up out of my sight.'

'Bollocks.'

'My sentiments exactly. You're stupid, leastways, you're acting stupid, and you're a mess and you're just giving it away. It's up to you, girl. You can either get yourself sorted or you can end up in a maisonette on Crown Leys with three kids and corned-beef legs. Please your bloody self, only don't think you're dragging the rest of us down with you. And especially not your sister. She's got a brain in her head.' *Gillian. So cool. Too cool for fifteen. Hard already, and resigned. How did that happen? Fifteen and settled for fuck all. Even given up on her typing. Dropping her knickers for some van driver. Quick, Ron, quick, pull them off. No. Not that. That's separate. This is Gillian, bunking off school because some horny bastard promised her a ring. She probably doesn't even enjoy it. Eileen never did. Just something you do to get a bloke, and you want it over and done quick. Mop up. Get back to your magazine. A few years and she'll be sitting in bed with her mail-order catalogues, choosing loose covers, doing it three times a month on Fridays. That's all it adds up to in the end.* 'Well you're going to school Monday anyway, and he's still banned. Now why don't you come downstairs and have a cup of tea and talk to your Mum?'

'I'm stopping up here.'

Good. I've had enough of your thick sulky face anyway. 'Suit yourself.'

Ronnie, beaten, taking the stairs slowly, flopping down a step, thump, down a step, thump, his mind engaged by this question: of Vic Shires and Raymond Pearce, which was most likely to be Nob-Head, and which was most likely to be Dick-Face?

J ack's bedroom. Grey and silky, big enough for a bowling alley. And twin beds. Annette's Mum was right.

Ronnie and Jack, wrapped around one another, warm and easy, under cover of a white cotton sheet.

'I'd begun to think you hadn't got a bed.'

'Yes, I could see it was bothering you.'

'No, well, I'd begun to think you kipped behind that settee every night.'

'I just like doing it fast with my clothes on. Don't you like it that way?'

'Yeah, it's great. It's just not what I'm used to.' *This is how I really like it. In bed with a good hard boner and my socks off.*

Jack, burrowing in under the crook of his arm, smaller and softer and easier to hold than she has ever been before.

*   *   *

'What are you used to?'

'Ah, you know. The usual.'

'There's no such thing as the usual. Tell me. I love knowing what other people do. I'll tell you about me and Tony. OK. About twice a year he comes home with a bottle of scent and six long-stemmed roses and he says "About time we had a fire-drill, pumpkin." '

'Pumpkin?'

'It's a nickname. Don't interrupt. Then he has a bath and a shave . . .'

'Hang on, hang on. Fire-drill?'

'Checking that everything's in working order. His equipment. All present and correct.'

'Right.'

'That's his way of pretending he doesn't use it and it might have gone rusty.'

'Right. But he does use it?'

'Of course he does. He diddles his secretary. In the car. Over the desk. Round at her place when her mother's asleep.'

'Oh my God. And you know all about it?'

'Of course.'

'And you don't mind?'

'Not at all. Her name's Audrey, and she's waiting for him.'

'Waiting for him to what?'

'Marry her. Anyway. So he has a bath and a shave, and then he slides his bed across next to mine, and all the while he's got this very solemn face on him as though he's going up for Communion, and his frankfurter's hanging out of his pyjamas . . .'

'Is he going to?'

'What?'

'Marry her?'

'Are you crazy? Stop interrupting. I'm getting to the best bit. And then he lowers himself down onto me with his cock still at half-mast, and he puts it in like he's connecting the tubes on a vacuum cleaner, you know, guiding it in, very carefully, and then

186

he slides it in and out, with his lips pursed, as if he's in absolute bloody agony, slides it in and out, never makes a sound until the very last second and then he says, "Oh dear." Then he pulls it out, very carefully, as if he's worried about snagging it on something, and he lies on his back for about ten minutes, looking at the ceiling. Then he says, "Well, that was very satisfactory. All seems to be in working order. A little nightcap for me, I think. Anything for you?'

'And that's twice a year?'

'Pretty well.'

'How can he have a beautiful wife like you and not want you all the time?'

'Do you want your wife all the time?'

'No.'

'Of course you don't. Wives aren't for wanting. And he's got Audrey. She plays golf. She knows about exchange rates.'

'So why doesn't he make it official. Why doesn't he go off and move in with her?'

'Because then he'd have to find another Audrey. You don't understand. It's not about *being* with somebody. It's about not having to be with somebody. Having a choice. And having a secret. It's about that too. Your turn now. Tell me about you and Eileen.'

'Well, compared with you and Tony, me and Eileen are at it all the time.'

'Tell me, tell me.'

'Once a week. Fridays. But obviously not if she's got her whassisname, or if she's got a cold or anything.'

'Ever done it on a Tuesday?'

Laughter, welling up fast, caught by Jack and cross-infecting them into a bellyache of agony.

'Stop it.'

'Can you credit unused ones? If you didn't fancy it one Friday, could you have it put by for Sunday?'

187

'Stop it.'

'What if you've got a stiffy on a Thursday? Can't you have one on account?'

'Stop it.'

'Carry on. Fridays. Right. Compose yourself. Does she remind you what day of the week it is?'

'She warns me if I'm not getting any.'

'That's thoughtful. Yes?'

'So, I get into bed.'

'Yes? Come on.'

'I can't.'

'Yes you can. I did, so now you've got to. You get into bed and . . . Eileen says, "Take me roughly, Big Boy." '

Laughter surfacing again fast, eyes still brimming, everything, anything, seeming funny.

'I get into bed, and Eileen fetches a towel. To save the sheets.'

'Aaargh. No. You have to do it on a towel?'

'An old one, that doesn't matter. And she likes it over as quick as possible. And no noise.'

'Nightie?'

'Yep.'

'Keeps it on?'

'Yep?'

'Missionary?'

'What's that?'

'You on top.'

'Yep.'

'And what does she do?'

'Don't know. Nothing. Holds her nightie out of the way.'

'Do you enjoy it?'

' 'S all right.'

'Better than nothing?'

'Yeah.'

'But not better than this?'

'Don't be daft. Nothing's better than this.'

'Tell me.'

'Well. You know?'

'Tell me.'

'Well . . . you want it. I can feel you wanting it. I've never had that.'

'Ah, come on.'

'I haven't. Well, maybe once. There was this Wren in Rosyth. Put my hand inside her knickers. But never with Eileen. I mean, she wouldn't refuse me, but there's never anything happening for her, you know? She'd sooner be getting on with her knitting.'

'She doesn't come?'

'No, no.' *Does she?*

'What a waste.'

'It's just how she is.'

'I suppose. Here. Look at this.'

Jack, springing up, naked, showing her long perfect back and her dancer's legs with the dimpled, leathery skin of a woman who could be forty, but probably is more. Ron, following her, pressing against her, but relaxed, looking over her shoulder into the open dressing-table drawer at perfume boxes, still in their cellophane.

'Is this what he brings you?'

'Yes.'

'*Antilope.* Never heard of it. You've got plenty. How many years' worth is this?'

'God knows. I can't stand the stuff.'

'Why does he keep bringing it?'

'That's Tony. Not very adventurous. Fucks like he's threading a needle and the only scent he buys is *Antilope*.'

'He goes to Singapore though.'

'You don't need to be adventurous to go to Singapore.'

'No? Funny name. *Antilope*.'

'Reminds him of Africa.'

'Does he go there too?'

'*Comes* from there, sweetie. Rhodesia. Came over in '31.'

Bloody hell. I was at Medway Street Mixed Infants in 1931. She can't be as old as him. She could be. Maybe it's all true. About the daughter and everything. Rhodesia. Is that near South Africa?

'Have you ever been there?'

'Yes. We lived there. I went back with him for a while. We had a bungalow in Gwelo. We've lived in lots of places.'

'Do you think you'll ever go back?'

'Rhodesia? Never. There's going to be trouble with the darkies.'

Ask her. Go on. 'Has he still got family out there?'

The smallest flicker. Something. Nothing.

'I guess we've all got family somewhere. Who cares. Put your trousers on and come into the sitting-room.'

'Yeah, I know. Time I was getting on.'

'No. Not that. Plenty of time for that. I'm going to teach you the tango.'

'What, now?'

'I thought you wanted dancing lessons.'

'I do. Ah Jack, you've got such a bum on you. I wish I could draw it. Such a bum. And your skin tastes of something.'

'Camay?'

'No, something nice. It's like biting into butter, only it's got something tart about it as well. A bit like a Cox's apple.'

'I don't like Cox's apples. Put your trousers on before I change my mind.

'Jack?'

The sitting-room, dust-sheeted and empty, with a tango playing on the Decca radiogram.

*   *   *

190

'Jack?'

'Stay there. I'm in the kitchen getting something. Don't come in. It's a surprise.'

Ronnie Glover, back in his boiler suit, clown-tangoing with an invisible partner.

'Excellent. You don't need lessons.'

Jack, with a can of fruit and a spoon, and a brown paper parcel under her arm.

'Eyes closed.'

'What is it?'

'Eyes closed, mouth open. I'm going to put something in your mouth and I want to know if it tastes like my skin. OK?'

'OK.'

Sweetness first. Too sweet. Then flesh, dissolving fast, in a sharp, buttery melt.

'Lovely. Is it peaches?'

'No. Anything like me?'

'Exactly like. They've tinned you, Jack. *Jack's Bum in Syrup*. Every Sunday teatime there's men pouring Carnation over your bum and eating it. What is it?'

'Taste some more. Have a guess.'

' 'S lovely. Well whatever it is they don't have it at the Co-op. And it's definitely not peaches?'

'No.'

'Where's it from?'

'Can't see. West Africa.'

'Give up.'

'Mango.'

'Never heard of it. Let's have a look. Looks like peaches.'

'And this is for you.'

'What for?'

191

'For your birthday, because I might not see you, if Tony's back, and because it's something I want you to have.'

Ronnie, scrabbling with brown paper and Sellotape, knowing already what is inside his parcel. *Plate of Figs* by Luca Dessi.

'I can't have this.'
   'You've got it now. It's yours.'
   'But you love it.'
   'I've had it long enough. You stop seeing paintings when you live with them. You just walk past them. So it's your turn now.'
   'Ah Jack. It's great. Great. What about Tony?'
   'What?'
   'He'll wonder where it's gone.'
   'Tony? In the kitchen? Noticing the walls?'
   'Yeah.'
   'No.'
   'Ah, it's brilliant. I've been trying to paint one for myself ever since I saw this. I asked Markham to try and get me some figs but he never did. But this is brilliant.'
   'Can you manage it on your bike?'
   'Yeah, easy. Ah, thanks, Jack.'
   'No. Happy Birthday. And thank *you*.'
   'What for?'
   'For being sweet. Being lovely. Letting me ride on top. Let's tango. And, turn, walk left, walk right, side left, close right, and again, turn, walk left, walk right . . .'

A housepainter with mango juice on his chin and a woman in a woollen dressing-gown, dancing to 'La Cumparsita', avoiding a pasting table on trestles and two excited poodles.

*   *   *

'When's Tony back?'
    'Two days.'
    'Right.'

A thin, icy finger curling round the gut. Then gone. Almost.

'I can do trees.'

'They don't have trees in *Cinderella*.'

'They must do.'

'No. Think about it. Where would you have trees in *Cinderella*? You have a kitchen. And you have a palace ballroom. Right?'

'Yeah, but . . .'

'Right.'

Raymond Pearce and Ronnie Glover, in St Columba's Church Hall, awaiting instructions from their technical and artistic director, Barry. Barry, trying to co-ordinate scenery painting, a costume call for adult leads, and the application of a Vicks anti-catarrh stick.

'Mrs Carver, if you please. Can we please do it in this order. Thin Ugly Sister first because he's badly parked. Then Cinderella and Prince Charming as quick as possible because the buses are terrible at this time of night. And then Fat Ugly Sister, Buttons,

194

Fairy Godmother. Lovely. Now how many painters do we have? Are you both painters? Two, plus Norman when he gets here. Well you'll be working on this flat. Palace Exterior. Norman's started drawing it out, you can see. Windows, archway, bit of a tree over here. So that's what's to be done, but let Norman start you off. He'll be along directly.'

'See?'
   'What?'
   'They are having a tree.'

'Hello, hello, hello. Anything doing? Ay up, mate. What are you doing here? Bloody hell, fancy bumping into you. Do you know, I always did think you'd make a lovely woman.'

'Ah God, it's Shires. It's Vic.'

'He said he might look in.'

'How does he know that Ugly Sister? Shires? How do you know that Ugly Sister?'

'Ron? Pearcie? All right then? Only I thought I'd drop in. See if you needed any advice. That's Weasel over there in the frock. His Dad used to have the allotment next to Jean's Dad. We've known him years. I never knew he did theatricals though. What's this you're doing?'

'Palace Exterior. Ron's doing the windows and I'm doing leaves.'

'That must make a change, Glover. Painting windows. Bloody busman's holiday for you. I should have thought you'd have done leaves and that, being artistic.'

'I didn't get much say in it. Pearce bagsied the tree before I could even open my mouth. Christ my neck's aching.'

'You want to give it a rest. Good God, look at the thighs on that. Get one of those across you, you wouldn't get up in a hurry. What part's she playing then?'

'Keep your voice down. Anyway, I thought you admired the larger woman?'

'I do. I am. Do you want a hand then?'

'Not for us to say. You'd better report to Barry. There's not that much to do really. Not without getting in each other's way. There's a bloke called Norman as well, only he keeps disappearing. Ask Barry if you're that keen. He's the one with the Vicks stick.'

'No, I'll leave it. I'll get off home now I've checked the quality of your work. Unless there's any more thighs I ought to have a look at. Hello. Here's your lady in the camel coat, Glover. Your lady from Gartree Road.'

Jack, hair tied back, coat slung round her shoulders, arms full of shopping bags. Ronnie, heart leaping from his chest, trying to be busy, or invisible, or dead normal.

'Mrs Carver. I was afraid I'd miss you. I've brought you the pink and the white for the Confetti chorus, and some grey for the mice, but not enough for all of them because this was the end of the roll. They've ordered some more for me and it'll be in next week.'

'It might not match.'

'Doesn't matter. Mice don't need to match. But what I am wondering about is what we can use for their tails.'

'Leave it to me.'

'Can I? But they do need to be good, strong, long tails, so they can swing them about when they're dancing.'

'Leave it to me. I've done tails before.'

'Oh well, that's marvellous. A relief.'

'What's happening about the bluebird costumes?'

197

'Damn and blast it. I knew there was something else. Tomorrow. Weekend at the latest. I'll get something.'

'Why don't you let me get it?'

'Would you? Mrs Carver, you're an angel. A life-saver. Money.'

Jack, peeling pound notes off a big fat roll, pushing back a strand of hair, aware of a man who is positioning himself for conversation.

'Evening.'

'Hello. How much do you think it'll be? Will this be about right?'

'Plenty.'

'Do you think so? Phone me if it's more. Bless you, Mrs C. I don't know where I'd be without you. Yes. Sorry? Hello.'

'Vic Shires. Friend of Ron Glover. We did meet. The other Sunday, when you were after him for a bit of paperhanging?'

'Oh yes. Hello.'

Shut up, Shires, you stupid pushy bastard. Why should she remember you. She's just being polite. Act ordinary. 'Hello.'

'Hello, Ron. I wondered if you'd be here. Brought some friends along with you?'

'Just young Raymond. I thought it'd keep him off the streets. Vic's just going.' *Go, you bastard. Stop hanging about.*

'I hear you're a dancing teacher, Jackie?'

'That's right.'

'I used to do a bit of dancing myself.'

'Yes?'

'And I was thinking I could do with brushing up a bit. We're having a little dinner-dance for our anniversary, and I was thinking . . .'

Go home, you interfering bastard. Stay away from my Jack.

'Well I don't have any ballroom classes at the moment, but I'll always do private lessons if someone asks. I could do you a private refresher. Ron can give you my number.'

Go home, Shires. I bloody hate you.

'Definitely, Jackie. Consider it a deal. I'll be in touch. The quickstep was always my forte. Fish Taii. Whisk and Syncopated Chasse . . .'

'Sounds as though you don't need much help from me.'

Yeah. You tell him, Jack. Piss off, Shires. Jack's mine. You wouldn't believe what I've done with that woman. That actual woman. So just pissing well piss off.

'Always room for improvement though, eh? That's what I always say. Nice to meet you again, anyway.'

'Yes. Indeed. Well, I must fly. Ron, Tony does like the stripes but he thinks we should have one contrasting wall. Something plain. You'll know what to do. Come and see me after the weekend?'

'Monday evening?'

'Perfect. Bye.'

Yeah, off you go, Jack. I don't like seeing you here. Stacked chairs. Smell of old shoes. Don't like people not knowing. That woman puts my old feller in her mouth and she really really likes it. Get that, Shires. And Barry. And Mrs Whassername. I've seen that woman without a stitch on her. Yeah, you and who else? The plumber? The bloke who reads the leccy meter? Ah, shut up. It's not like that. You're special. Who says? She didn't. She's never said anything like that. And what have you got? A few shags while he's in Singapore? Then what? And what happens when you run out of rooms to decorate? You won't be able to just go there, without a job to do. It'll finish. And it won't bother her. She won't cry or anything, or say she wants it to carry on, whatever it takes. She might. She won't. How could it? You couldn't even see her, just to go to the pub or have a bit of a cuddle somewhere. Nothing. You've got nothing. Shires has got more than you. He's got a wife he really likes going home to.

'You're quiet, Glover.'

'Ah, sod this. I'm packing in. Painting bloody windows. I've been painting windows all day.'

'That's what I said.'

'Do you want to swap for a bit, Ron? I'll do the window and you do the tree? If you like?'

'No. You're all right, Pearce. I'm off home. Leave you to it.'

'You're not abandoning the lad?'

'Why not?'

'Well, you brought him. He don't know anybody.'

'I don't know anybody. Don't make any difference. Good grief, I was being torpedoed by Germans when I was his age.'

'Pardon me for breathing.'

'I'm not his bloody mother, you know?'

'Have you got the hump because he's doing leaves and you're doing windows?'

'Don't be so childish.'

'Have I done something wrong, Ron?'

Raymond Pearce, with green paint on his shirt and his Adam's apple working anxiously.

'No. Course you haven't, lad. He's just got the hump about something. He'll be all right in the morning. I'll stop with you if you like. I'll do some knotty bits on the tree trunk if you've got any black.'

'Don't know, Vic. We'd better ask permission first.'

Ronnie, cycling through a fine, cold drizzle, going home to Eileen, in her brown jumper and her fluffy slippers. Home, for another row about Gillian under that big bright living-room light, far away from Jack's low, pink lamps and glasses of cold, greenish wine.

Behave like that again and Shires'll suspect something. Wish he knew. That'd show him. Mr Bloody Wall Lights. No. Vic wouldn't be impressed. He just talks about stuff. He wouldn't ever do anything. He loves his Jean. I love my Jack. Wish I could tell somebody. It's not real if nobody knows. Tony'd move out. I'd move in. Me and Jack. What are you like? Some woman's bit on

200

the side, just while there's decorating needs doing. Then you'll be out on your ear. Then you'll never see her again. You'll hear Susan talking about Madame, but you'll never see her. Course you will. She gave you a painting. That's special. That's got to mean something. Yeah. But it's not enough. It's not. A painting's not waking up in the morning with her bum tucked close to your belly, and making her a cup of tea, and watching her comb her hair. Tony can do that, but you can't. And you never, never, never will. You're crap, Glover. You can't draw. You've forgot all that Italian you learned. You're just a runty little housepainter on a bike. You're nothing. And you're on your own. All on your own.

Ronnie, something hungry and vile worming inside him, swelling till it fills his whole chest, pedalling faster, away from the silence of wet empty streets and the terror of something that is gaining on him fast.

You run straight home else the Ten O'Clock Horses'll get you. Listen. Can you hear them? I can. They're on the way, so straight home and don't look behind you. I've told you what happens if you look behind. 'Ah, come on, Glover. It's only twenty to nine.'

'W here is he?'

'Amsterdam. No. Jersey. Amsterdam's next week. Let's go and do it in the car.'

'How do you mean?'

'Let's drive out somewhere quiet and do it in the back of the car.'

What if somebody sees us? What if Susan gets run over and Eileen needs me in a hurry and I'm not here paperhanging like I'm supposed to be? 'Yeah. If you like.'

'You don't want to.'

'It's not that exactly. I just like it here. I like being snuggled up with you.'

'Yes, you do, don't you. I've never really come across that in a man before. Quick pee and a cigarette and they usually like to be tucking their shirt-tails in.'

'Do they? I thought they fell asleep.'

'What do you do at home? Do you have to get up and put the towel in the laundry basket?'

'I wish I'd never told you about the towel. You must think I'm a right pillock.'

'No.'

'Well why keep bringing it up then?'

'All right, all right. Keep your hair on. I was only teasing. And I don't think you're a pillock. I think you're great.'

'Yeah.'

'You don't fancy it in the car then?'

'Not compared to this.'

'You're not bored?'

'I'm never bored.' *You're bored when it's the Black and White Minstrels on the telly and it's too cold to go down the shed.*

'There aren't many people who can say that.'

'Are you bored?' *She's bored. She's bored with you. This is it. You're getting the elbow. Might not even get paid for the job.*

'I do get bored. Not with you though.'

'Yeah?'

'No. You're such a turn-up. You look so straight and yet you're so funny. You kill me. And you're shy about it. That's what's so sweet. Most men are drunk on themselves.'

That's Shires she's talking about. Ha. And Tony.

'But you're not. You're a breath of fresh air. I think it's a working-class thing. Would you say most working-class men are like you?'

'Don't know. I didn't know class had anything to do with it. I thought the pillocks and bastards were pretty well spread.' *Working fucking class.*

'You're not offended that I called you working class?'

'No. I've never thought about it.'

'I've offended you. I can tell.'

'No. I couldn't care less what people call me, Jack. I mean, I am working class. Still shave in the kitchen sink if Eileen's not around. Still go to the Co-op for the divi. Still got coal in the bath and a whippet in the backyard. But I do know there's other ways of living. You know? I think about stuff, all about things I've never tried, and learning things, and being better this year than I was last year, knowing more and making things happen, instead of just staying stuck. So what class does that make me? I mean, a lot of this working-class business gets up my nose. Like, if you're down you'd better stay down and be cheerful about it. Like down's the only decent thing to be. Or the ones who think if you get carpet in your bathroom you're a fucking overnight aristocrat, even if your mind's still full of crap and you're reading the *Express* on Sundays. I don't know about class, Jack, but there's a lot of very ignorant people about. And lazy. That bothers me. Our Gillian's ignorant. And she's going to get ignoranter and ignoranter. As long as she's got batteries for her tranny she'll be satisfied. Eh? No curiosity. If God himself dropped in she wouldn't come to the foot of the stairs to have a look. My Susan's not like that. Always on the go. Always asking. Me, I'm buggered if I know where I fit in. Down the shed. Yeah. Shed Class, that's me.'

'You fit in here. Here. Here. Fit in here. Doesn't matter you're not hard. Ah, you're sweet. Sweet.'

'Where would we have gone? If we'd gone out in the car?'

'Anywhere. A dark lane.'

'What if somebody looked in?'

'In a dark lane on a cold wet night? Give them a treat I should think. What are you doing for your birthday?'

'Don't know. Eileen's on about going to the Wheatsheaf. Taking the girls, Saturday night.'

'Nice. How old are you going to be?'

'Not telling you.'

'Thirty-six?'

'Thirty-eight. When's your birthday?'

'June tenth. Not telling you.'

'Thirty-six?'

'Flatterer. It doesn't bother you, does it? The age difference?'

'Don't think about it.' *Liar.* 'It's not that much, anyway.' *You haven't got a bloody clue how much it is.* 'You're a very beautiful woman, Jack. It wouldn't bother me if you were fifty.' *Fuck. Fifty was the wrong one to say. Too close. Should have said sixty. But nobody'd believe you if you said sixty because sixty's horrible. Liver spots. Turkey throat. Fuck. She's fifty. Could be more. What does fifty look like? Drop it.* 'What shall we do when you've run out of rooms that need decorating?'

'Well, first I shall have all of the outside painted. Then I'll set fire to the kitchen, so that'll need doing again. And we'll just carry on like that. Like one of those long bridges where the painters get to the end and have to go straight back to the beginning. Or, I'll come round to your house and say, "Excuse me, Mrs Glover, but can your husband come out to play?"'

'Don't joke about it. It'll be really difficult. I mean, I can't just come round. I've got to have a reason.'

'Relax. You could get a gold medal for worrying.'

'I know.' *But it's all right for you, Jack. Your life's sorted, and I'm just the cherry on the top. We're not even. Your life's brilliant. Mine's shite.*

'You could turn pro.'

'Yeah?'

'Put an advert in the paper. Ron Glover, For All Your Worrying Requirements . . .'

'Yeah.'

'No Problem Too Small.'

'**M**a?'

'Oh it's you. Eileen was in earlier.'

'Yeah? Where's Pop?'

'Wandering.'

'Is he all right?'

'Right as he'll ever be. He keeps wandering off. Eileen says he ought to have tests done, but I can't be bothered. I'm glad to see the back of him. He's no company for me. I'd like to get a little cat only we're not allowed.'

'How about a budgie?'

'You're allowed budgies. No point though. I shan't be here much longer and then who'd look after it? You'd end up with it. No. Let him wander. Her next door doesn't help. She keeps having him in, doing jigsaws. If anybody should have him doing jigsaws it should be me.'

'Would you like a jigsaw?'

'No thank you. Here you are then. Happy Birthday. I haven't wrapped them. Waste of money.'

'Thanks. Cuff-links. Thanks.'

'Do you remember them? You and Eileen gave them to him one Christmas. It's all right. He's never even had them out of the box. You might as well have them. It saved me worrying what to get you.'

'Yeah, I wouldn't have wanted you doing that.'

'Don't you like them?'

'No. Yes. They're lovely. Cheers, Ma.'

'Eileen asked about Christmas. Said we were invited as per.'

'Yeah. Course.'

'We'll come for our dinner, but we won't stop. We'll get back while it's still light. You never know who's roaming the streets once it's dark.'

'But it gets dark about three. We shall hardly be finished dinner. What did Eileen say?'

'She said we should stop for our tea and get a taxi.'

'I agree with her.'

'We can't pay out for taxis. We've only got the pension, you know?'

'For crying out loud, Ma, when have we ever expected you to fork out for taxis? Come for your dinner, have your tea, watch a bit of telly and then get a taxi. We'll book it. We'll pay for it. And did she tell you about the telephone?'

'Yes. You must have money to burn.'

'No. If people can phone me up, about decorating jobs, it'll make us money. Pay for itself. See? Like Miss Lockwood up near the golf-course? She's always wanting bits doing, and she has to come trailing round and hope to catch somebody in. But once we're on the blower, no problem. You've got to do it, Ma, if you're in business.'

'Oh well, of course I wouldn't know. I'm just a pensioner.'

'Beryl next door's a pensioner. She's on the phone.'

'That's just swank.'

'Right. Anyway. They said three to six weeks. So we might be connected up by Christmas. You'll be able to have a go on it. You could phone Ivy in Kidderminster.'

Ma Glover, with her dry tight curls and her old lady smell, dismissing telephones, Christmas, and sisters who live in Kidderminster with an unpleasant click of her dentures.

'Don't go without your cuff-links.'

'What, no fry-up?'

'You don't have fry-ups when you're going out to a restaurant.'

'But I'm hungry.'

'You can have a sandwich, or a biscuit.'

'But I'm properly hungry. What's the point of having a birthday tea if you can't have what you want?'

'And what do you want?'

'A fry-up.'

'No. I'll do you egg on toast.'

'Egg on dippy?'

'Go on then. But don't you dare tell me you're stuffed when we're out tonight. I want it to be really nice.'

'It will be. I won't be. Two eggs?'

'No wonder you're getting a gut on you. You're going like Pop.'

'Eileen?'

'Yeah?'

Take this slowly, Glover. Proceed with caution. 'I've got this painting I've come by. I'd quite like to put it up.'

'Yeah?'

'Yeah. Madame gave it to me. She was having a clear-out. Didn't want it any more.'

'Where is it?'

Down the shed.'

'What's it of?'

'Fruit.'

'Sounds nice. Yeah if you like. As long as it's not got any bare bottoms in it?'

'No.' *Well that wasn't difficult. Now change tack.* 'What have I got to wear tonight?'

'A tie.'

'Yeah? How about cuff-links?'

'You haven't got any.'

'I have now. Birthday present from Ma, lovingly selected from a drawer full of Pop's old Christmas presents. I wouldn't mind, only we gave them to him. And the thing of it is, why ever did we give them to him? He's in that old ganzie every day, and a sports shirt. And I'm in a vest and a boiler suit. This family has got no need of cuff-links whatsoever and I end up getting them for my birthday.'

'Ah, take no notice. Where's this painting then?'

'I'll fetch it, shall I?'

'Yes. And I'm only doing you one egg because we're going to be in company tonight.'

'I thought you said it was apples?'

'I said it was fruit.'

'What are they?'

'Figs.'

'Funny looking things.'

Don't push it. 'Well if you don't like it . . .'

'No, it's all right. You can put it up. I'd just sooner have had apples.'

'Where's it from, Dad?'

210

'Madame was having a clear-out. It used to hang in her kitchen.'

'Pictures? In a kitchen?'

'Yes.'

'She evidently doesn't do a lot of cooking. You don't have paintings in a proper kitchen.'

'Annette's Mum's got a shopping-list board in her kitchen and you can wipe it clean and keep using it over and over. Are we all having egg and dippy?'

'No, just your father because he's a rumblegut. Now I'm going for a bath and then you and Gillian are having my water, so sort out who's having it first, and we're going from here at seven o'clock. You can have a sandwich or a biscuit and then you're to save yourself for your dinner.'

'Dad?'

'Yeah?'

'Where are you going to put that picture?'

'Somewhere in the living-room. I don't think your Mum wants it in her kitchen.'

'Dad?'

'Yeah?'

'Do you like Madame?'

'She's all right.'

'I don't think she's very polite.'

'Why's that?'

'Because I heard her say to Mrs Stockwell, "It's my money he plays with. When I married him he didn't have a pot to piss in." That's not very nice, is it?'

'You shouldn't have been earwigging.'

'Dad?'

'Yeah?'

'I'm going to have steak tonight.'

'Me too.'

Saturday night at the Wheatsheaf Berni. Its windows onto Wellington Street touting views of green-stemmed wineglasses and pink serviettes and a great roaring fire in the Rutland Lounge, where you may relax and enjoy an aperitif or something from the extensive range of liqueur coffees. People hurrying by in macs, to the pub, to the Gaumont to see *Prisoner of Zenda*, to An Evening of Clairvoyance with Ethel Smith. People, other people, turning proudly under the coachyard arch towards the hum and tinkle of the Surf 'n' Turf Restaurant, in a sweat over wining and dining and whether you're supposed to hang up your own coats or give them to the waiter to take.

'It's nice, isn't it?'
  'Very nice. What's it to be? Steak and chips four times?'
  'I think we're supposed to have a drink first. A glass of sherry, while we're deciding.'
  'Yeah, course. If you like. Is that what you'd like. A sherry?'
  'Yes.'

'Have we got to have sherry, Dad?'

'No. You'll have Pepsi. Do I have to go and get them from the bar?'

'I don't think so. Keep your voice down. Somebody'll come in a minute.'

'Sorry. How am I supposed to know?'

'Sir?'

'Oh, right. Right. A Pepsi for Susan. Gillian? You want a Pepsi? Another Pepsi. A sherry for the wife . . .'

'Dry, medium or sweet, sir?'

'Which would you like, Eileen?'

'What do you think, Ron?'

'How about medium?'

'Yes.'

'And I'll have half of bitter.'

'Certainly, sir.'

'Ron. You don't have bitter in a place like this. You should have had a sherry.'

'I don't like sherry.'

'Neither do I, but that's not the point.'

'Bollocks.'

A smile from Gillian. First sighting in weeks.

'Nice lighting, isn't it? Subdued. I'd like us to have it like this at home. Two or three little lamps instead of that great big bulb beating down in the middle.'

'No good if you've got mending to do. You need a proper light for mending. It is nice though. How the other half lives, eh?'

'It doesn't have to be the other half. People say that, but for a lot of things you're just in the half you choose. I mean, you don't have to win the pools to have a few table lamps or come out to a place like this once in a while. You just have to get yourself organized. You've got to think how you want things to be and if it's money that's stopping you, just start putting a bit by. Bung

213

your loose change in a jar every night and after a few weeks, Bob's your uncle. See, when you think what people spend in the boozer, over a weekend say, and add that up over the weeks, this is nothing. You don't have to be royalty to have a steak dinner from time to time. You've got to decide what you want and go after it. Either that or you end up like Norrie Chater, pissing it away in the Gents' and hating the bosses. It's about mentality, Eileen. If you want table lamps and steak dinners, you've just got to get yourself organized.'

'As long as I can keep my big light for mending. Well I'll be jiggered.'

'What?'

'Over the other side. The woman in aquamarine and the man who looks like Tommy Trinder. That's Anne. From work. What a blooming cheek. She's only here because I said we were coming. That's just like her. Then on Monday she'll get it in first, bragging about it. She wouldn't even have thought of it if I hadn't said. She gets on my flipping pippin.'

'Never mind about her. Let's have some grub.'

Four prawn cocktails. Four T-bone steaks with French fries and selection of seasonal vegetables. A bottle of Blue Nun, and two more Pepsis.

'You ought to have a try of this, Gillian.'

'Why?'

'Because you should. You're nearly sixteen. You should have a try of wine. It's part of your education.'

'She's all right with her Pepsi.'

'Just a taste, Eileen. That's all I'm saying.'

'I'll have a taste, Dad.'

'You will not. She will not, Ron.'

'Ah, go on. A taste never hurt anybody. Go on, Gillian. You have a sip of your Mum's and Susan can have a sip of mine.'

'It's horrible. Bitter.'

'No it's not. It's sour. I like it. It's a bit like vinegar.'

'Well just steady on. That's enough. How's your steak, Ron?'

'Lovely. How's yours?'

'Lovely. It's a real treat. Anyhow, happy birthday, and happy anniversary for when it comes.'

'Yeah, you too, darling.' *You lying cheating bastard.* 'Pop'd like it here.'

'Don't even think about it. I'd be having kittens in case he did something.'

'No, he'd love it. Ma wouldn't.' *Ma'd polish the knives and forks with her serviette and say the steaks were too pricey.* 'Steak all right, Gillian?'

' 'S all right.'

'You'll soon be able to bring us here. When you're working. Specially if you get your shorthand and typing. You'll be well away.'

'I'm not getting my shorthand and typing. I keep telling you that. I'm going into the Hosiery.'

'It'll drive you mad.'

'No it won't. It's better money and they have music on all day. I'm going to go to Ladies Pryde and be a finisher.'

'You sound like you've got it all worked out.'

'I have. And after I've paid Mum I'm going to save up and get driving lessons.'

'So am I. Next year.'

'Are you, Dad? And shall we be getting a car?'

'Eventually.'

'Brilliant.'

'It's all happening round the Glovers, isn't it? Gillian's going to need a bodyguard to bring her wages home. Susan'll go to college. Eileen's going to start night school and do shorthand and typing . . .'

'No I'm not. I've changed my mind. I'm going to do

215

Cake Decoration and Sugarcraft.'

'I stand corrected. And your old Dad's going to get a driving licence, do some more evening jobs, buy a little Ford, sort that shed out . . .'

'Knock through?'

'Yeah. Probably. What do you fancy for afters, girls?'

Three strawberry and vanilla ice-creams with Pompadour fan wafer. One apple pie and cream.

'I'm sorry, sir, we don't serve tea. We do coffees and liqueurs which we are pleased to serve, for your greater comfort, in the Rutland Lounge.'

'Right.' *For Christ's sake, Eileen. Fancy asking for tea.* 'You should go and say hello to your friend before we shift.'

'I will not. I shall pretend I never saw her.'

'Don't be so wet.'

'No. I shan't. I've never liked her. She's common. Always talking about her private life. Are you all right, Susan?'

'Yeah. Great.'

'She's had too much wine.'

'No I haven't. I like coming out for dinner. Dad? In the war, right, were you a hero?'

'No, darling. I was an engineer.'

'So if we get a car you'll know how to fix it?'

'Not really. Ships' engines are different.'

'Did you kill anybody?'

'No, darling.' *You don't know what you did. Not in the long run.* 'No, I just helped look after the turbines. Never knew what I was doing really. I just did as I was told.'

'Did anybody try to kill you?'

'Oh yes. I was on two boats that got hit. There were mines all over the place. Only none of them had my name on it, as it turned out. Else I dodged it. It might still be out there. Waiting for me to go on a day trip to Ostend.'

'Because if you'd have got killed, I wouldn't ever have been born, would I? Nor Gillian?'

'That's true.'

'Did anybody try to kill you, Mum?'

'Night after night. The sirens used to go and we'd have to get up and go off to the shelter. Your Nana and Grandad Barlow had an Anderson shelter in their garden. And we'd be down there all night sometimes, waiting for the All Clear, and you never knew what you were coming out to. You never knew if you'd got a home left to go to. They flattened Saxby Street one night and there was a lady that didn't like going down the shelters, all they ever found of her was her hand.'

'Where was the rest of her?'

'Squished all across the street.'

'Gillian! They just never found her, that's all.'

'Were you very frightened?'

'Not really. We got used to it, didn't we, Ron?'

I never. After I'd seen Ratcliffe jump in the water with his life-jacket on wrong and break his neck, I was scared fucking senseless. My legs wouldn't move. Sometimes they still won't. Ratcliffe didn't have some heavenly fucking aura round him. He was just that stupid git who thought he looked like Frank Sinatra. One minute he was there. The next minute he was gone. That's how it happens. And everything just carries on. When you go, it's just like a sparrow farting. 'No, well, you didn't always have time to be scared. It's later on. When you've got time to think. Are we going to have one of these Gaelic coffees, Eileen? Pop's always going on about them. He has them round at Beryl's, next door.'

'He does not. He goes to sleep and dreams half of the things he tells you. Gaelic coffee.'

'No. I've seen the whisky on the side. He's not as puddled as you make out. So shall we?'

'I shan't like it if it's too strong. Get one and one ordinary and I'll just have a sip. You look tiddly, young lady.'

'I'm not. What did you do in the war, Mum? Were you in the Munitions?'

'Lord no. I was biscuit-packing when I left school, and then when I was seventeen I went nursing at the Sparkenhoe. That was just for old people and people who'd been bombed out but weren't too bad. See, all the main nurses were needed for the troops.'

'What were the Munitions, Mum?'

'Very dangerous work, Susan. And some people's hair turned a funny yellow. You could get blown to smithereens.'

'You could be a nurse now, Mum. Why don't you? Be better than being a dinner lady.'

'No. I'd never do nursing again. It's horrible. You wouldn't believe some of the horrible things I had to do. Bathing old men. Cleaning up sick and worse than sick. And I wasn't much older than Gillian.'

'This is smashing, Eileen. Have a taste.'

'No, you have it. I'd sooner have had a cup of tea.'

Ronnie Glover, sipping hot spirity coffee, contented, full, aware that he has passed a whole evening with his wife and daughters without a cross word or any aching thoughts of Jack. Ronnie, observing through a light inebriate haze that even in high-heeled shoes his wife has no ankles, and that it is very very easy indeed to spend seventeen quid.

'Did you tip him?'

'Yes.'

'How much?'

'Never mind how much.'

'It's been lovely, hasn't it? Tip-top. Have you enjoyed it?'

'Yeah. We'll come again. After Christmas, when we've saved up.'

*　　*　　*

Eileen, on her feet at the third attempt, permitting a waiter to help her into her mac with the wary gratitude of a bitch having her bottom sniffed.

'I hope you weren't silly with the tip.'

'What do you generally get Jean for Christmas?'

'I don't. We always get something for the house.'

'You don't get her scent and stuff?'

'No. See, anything in that line, if she wants it, she goes out and gets it. She's earning. Same with me. If I fancy a new shirt or anything, I don't wait, you know, hoping I'll get one for Christmas. I send Jean for it. No, we like to get something for the house. We're getting a Kenwood Chefette. What are you getting Eileen?'

'I don't know. I never know what to get her.'

'Get her a Kenwood Chefette.'

'Yeah? What is it?'

'Food mixer. Does everything for you. All the different attachments. We saw it at the Ideal Home Exhibition. Brilliant.'

'No.'

'Something to wear?'

'Wouldn't know where to start.'

'A nice jumper. That'd be easy. Get it from Marks and keep the ticket, then she can take it back and change it.'

'Yeah?'

'Or bath cubes. They're very popular with the ladies.'

'Say you wanted to be dead romantic like, what would you get Jean?'

'How much are we spending?'

'Ten quid tops.'

'Can't be done, my old mate. I was going to say a ring. Eternity ring or something. But if you've only got a tenner I should just wrap it round your old feller and tie it with a ribbon. You got your Mam and Dad coming to you?'

'Supposed to be. Pop's game but Ma's dragging her feet. It's the same every bloody year. There's no buses running so they've got to get a taxi. I mean, they could walk. It's not out of the question. But a taxi's favourite and we're bunging for it, but every year we have to have this sod's opera about managing on the old-age pension and how you don't go throwing your money around when you're struggling to get through the week. And they're hardly speaking anyway. The only thing is, give them a drink as soon as they've got their coats off and keep them tanked up. I used to love Christmas, with the kiddies and that, but I hate it now. You could cancel it for me.'

'Yeah, I'm not fussed about it neither. But I could run them, you know? I have to get the motor out Christmas morning because we have this old lady from down the Belgrave Road. She's got ulcerated legs and her son's in Tasmania so we always have her. If I'm fetching her I could fetch your Mam and Dad and drop them off.'

'Yeah?'

'Yeah, no problem. He still giving you cause for concern, your Dad?'

'No. A lot of it's just got up by Ma and Eileen.'

'No, I meant him and his lady friend. Anyway. You tell them. I'll run them.'

'Cheers, Vic.'

'No problem, Ronald. No problem.'

Ronnie Glover, laid off early because of freezing fog, heading for town with ten pounds three shillings and sevenpence in his pocket and two women to buy for. Half-past three and nearly dark, but the streets and shops busy with laden hard-pressed women, frowning and pondering. A Turtle Wax and Chamois Leather Gift Set from Halford's Car Accessories? Or a Rael-Brook drip-dry shirt in lemon?

Ronnie, sleepwalking through Boots, along the aisle of Coty Luxury Gift Caskets and Perfect Gifts from Yardley, wanting to buy everything and nothing. Exciting, impossible ideas skittering across his mind. Something made of silk. Or leather. Something printed on thick creamy paper. Something perfect and unique for under a tenner, and small enough to hide in a shed and transport on a bike.

Ah, fuck it. I won't bother. I'm not turning up with six bath cubes just because it's Christmas. God. This time of year you can make a real idiot of yourself. No. Get something for Eileen and then go home.

Ronnie, creeping through the carpeted hush of Marshall and Snelgrove in his donkey jacket, in through Gloves & Belts and out through Fountain Pens, without a pause. Back on the street, lightheaded, the earaching cold coming too soon after a hot and airless store. Crossing the market, squeezing between the traders' vans, slipping on damp cabbage trimmings, drawn to the windows of the jewellers on the corner of Market Street by the sight of something magical. Among the cocktail watches and the musical jewellery boxes with little plastic ballerinas, pieces of rock, all sizes, cracked open like eggs, displaying their crystals in a thousand different flashes of purple.

'The rocks. In the window.'
  'What?'

'The rocks? The purple rocks in the window?'

'Yes?'

'What are they?'

'They're for display.'

'How much are they?'

'They're not for sale.'

'But how much would they be if they were?'

'They're just not.'

'Could you get me one that was for sale?'

'No.'

'Why's that?'

'Because they're for display purposes only.'

'Where do you get them from?'

'You'd have to ask the manager.'

'Yes?'

'He's not here.'

'Will he be here tomorrow?'

'Yes. But it won't make any difference. This is a jewellery shop.'

'Right.'

'And I'm in charge when he's not here, and I can tell you that we never sell those rocks.'

'Right.'

'We can only sell what's on our stock list, you see? That's our system.'

'Yep. Right. Well. Thank you very much.' *Fuck you very much.*

Ronnie Glover, suddenly getting a move on because he's had a good idea, buying a pair of pale blue fluffy size 6 slippers for his wife who takes a 4½, a thick pad of cartridge paper, ink, brushes, and a postcard of a painting of a woman, with a long back and a proper bum, stepping out of her wrap into a hip-bath.

*   *   *

Have Saturday afternoon down the shed. Try copying it freehand. If no good, trace it with a bit of Eileen's greaseproof. Put some long dark hair on it. Tell her it's a Ronnie Glover original. Yeah. Great. And money left over. Stacks. Could get a little frame for it, if it works out. And a bar of Fruit & Nut to eat on the way home. Yeah. Sorted.

T he last day of term. The dinner ladies of Southfields Secondary Modern sitting down to Cod and Potato Bake, mince pies and paper hats in a hall freshly mopped with Dettol and hot water. Connie, neat and nippy, with pretty white hair, who should really have retired but would miss it all so much, especially since Albert . . . Lilian, too bowed for fifty-something because she has a very big bosom and a mother who's eighty-seven and marvellous, who never believed in corsetry. Joyce, who's due to have all her teeth out, and Anne, who keeps herself looking nice but the roots of her hair are grey and the ends are chocolate brown. And Eileen, the baby, who sometimes wears eye-shadow and sometimes looks like a suet pudding, and is reliable as clockwork and works hard and nobody, nobody really likes.

'You got your bird yet, Anne?'

'No. He generally wins one. He gets tickets for all the draws. And if he don't we can always get a cockerel from my brother-in-law. You got yours?'

'No. We're going to our Pat's. I shall get a piece of pork for Boxing Day and that'll do us. Your sister coming to see you, Lilian?'

'We haven't heard anything. It's usually just Mother and me so I'll do a bit of chicken I expect. Take it off the bone. She doesn't eat much these days. As long as she's got the telly and her advocaat she'll be happy. There's a lot of nourishment in advocaat.'

'What are you doing, Connie?'

'Keeping a good fire burning. Having a little cry.'

'Ah, Connie. Come to us. Don't sit on your own.'

'Yes. Or come to us. I'm sure Mother wouldn't mind.'

'No thank you. I'd sooner be on my own.'

'Ah. It don't seem right. I'd go mad if I had to be on my own over Christmas. Mind you, I go mad anyway. He's completely kaylied from Christmas Eve morning till the booze runs out, and then you know what they're like after they've had sprouts. So if you want to keep me company, Connie, you're very welcome.'

'And I'd ask you, Connie, only we've got Ron's Ma and Pop coming. But Boxing Day. Why don't you come Boxing Day?'

'No thank you. It's only Christmas, you know? Nothing wrong with being alone with your memories and some nice buttery toast.'

'Oh no, I couldn't. I couldn't sit around, harking back on things, when everybody else is having a good time. You all ready, Eileen?'

'Just about. Ron's finishing Wednesday afternoon and he's got a little job to see to up Gartree Road on Thursday, so he's picking the bird up on his way home.'

'Every time I hear about your Ron he's up Gartree Road doing a little job.'

'I know. I told him he might as well move in there. Not really. She's nice though. Madame. Always got something needs seeing to, and she pays on the dot, cash in hand. That's the thing.'

'Don't it bother you?'

'What?'

'Him being round there so much. Round another woman's.'

'What? My Ron? You're joking. He's not like that. And she's

old. She's fifty if she's a day. Anyway, I've marzipaned the cake. And we've got the girls suede jackets out of my catalogue, so that's saved pushing round the shops. I just wish the telephone people'd come and get that done. They did say we might have it in for Christmas.'

'No, you won't have it for Christmas. Not now. They'll have all their jobs booked up till the New Year.'

'They might not. There's a few days yet.'

'I don't think so. See, we were very lucky. We got priority treatment with Len being on weekend call-out. We went straight to the top of the list.'

'How do you mean? On call-out?'

'To Daventry. Anything goes wrong with that transmitter, it's got to be fixed, day or night.'

'But he only works in the canteen.'

'Don't make no difference. People've got to be fed. That's the thing. If your work's of an urgent nature, you get priority treatment.'

'It doesn't bother me actually. It might be a nuisance. People ringing up all over Christmas wanting to book Ron for decorating.'

'Perhaps you could swing it, Eileen? Tell the phone people your Ron is on call, day and night, to Gartree Road. Work of an urgent nature, eh?'

*N*early Christmas. Five days off work because of how it falls. Two nice little paperhanging jobs lined up for January. Eileen's happy. Gillian's better than she was. And we've got a whole long evening, supposed to be painting a door where the dogs have scratched it, and Tony's definitely, definitely away. Life's good. I'm probably going to get a blow-job with the lights on. Life's bloody perfect.

Ronnie, freewheeling down Narborough Hill with a freshly washed dick and a commendable drawing of a naked woman's back, traced from a postcard and finished in ink.

Jack, hair up, lipsticked, standing in the doorway in a black fur coat.

'You're going out?'
  'Come in for heaven's sake. You're letting all the warmth out.'
  'Have you just got in?'
  'Where's the paint?'

228

You know I haven't brought paint. You know what I'm here for. Why are you being like this? Tony. He's here. 'Tony's back then?'

'Come through so we can discuss what it is I want you to do.'

Jack. Don't be like this. It's our last time before Christmas. I've done you a drawing. 'I'd better give you this now.'

'What is it?'

'For Christmas.'

'How sweet. I'll save it for Christmas Day.'

'I don't think you'd better. It's just a little drawing I did.' *Took all of Saturday afternoon.*

'I'm sure I'll love it. Now look. You can see what these naughty girls have done to the inside of this door. So if you could do something with it? Just until we get round to doing this room properly?'

Ah fuck, Jack. Fucking fuck. What's going on?

'Is something wrong?'

'Why?'

'You look like you lost a shilling and found sixpence.'

'Yeah?'

'Want your Christmas present?'

'Yeah?'

'Do you remember?'

'What?'

'When we were talking once, about what we'd really like, what really turned us on? Remember? About the coat?'

'What? A woman with just a fur coat on? Ah, Jack. What, really? You've got nothing on under there?'

'Come and find out.'

'Ah my God. It *is* Christmas. It's bloody fantastic yippee-ay-aye Christmas.'

Ronnie, joy returned, finding Jack in silk and lace and stocking tops inside her soft black coat and taking her, fast and confident, with short, sharp yelps. Ronnie, imagining he might rise to this pleasure again and again through the long December evening, but spent, unable to resist a narcoleptic drowse, slobbering a little from the corner of his mouth onto his hand and a label that says MISHKIN FURRIERS, SOUTH MOLTON STREET.

'Merry Christmas.'

'Sorry? What? Sorry?'

'I said, Merry Christmas.'

'I'm sorry. I dropped off. Would you like some more?'

'No, I'm just fine thank you. I opened my envelope.'

'Yeah?'

'It's very good. You're very good.'

Yeah. Good with tracing paper and half a drawing pad screwed up on the floor of the shed because it kept going wrong. 'I couldn't think what else I could get you.'

'It's lovely. Very special. You'll have to draw the other side of me some time. I could sit for you.'

Oh yeah.

'Did you like your present?'

'Best ever.'

'Sure?'

'Sure.'

'There's still time for me to get you some socks if you'd rather.'

'No, you're all right. This'll do.'

'This was easier to wrap.'

'Yeah.'

'Didn't need any Sellotape.'

'No.'

'Didn't have to get Tony to put his finger on the knot.'

'No.'

Ronnie, restored by laughter, rolling her over, taking the last few pins from her hair, looking at the tawny bits round the pupils of her eyes and the little lines from the nose down to the corners of her mouth.

*   *   *

'Jack?'

'Mm?'

'You're the dog's bollocks.'

'My God. You don't just hang good wallpaper and draw nudes and fuck like a demon. You're a poet as well.'

'T hen we sing this song, about stars and dreams and that. I'll sing it to you if you like. Grandad? Are you listening? And then we do our dance only I'm not showing you that while Gillian's watching. You're only jealous. Mum, she's doing it again. She's giving me a look. Then Cinderella sings her bit. It's called "The Second Star To The Right", and then we throw all this glittery stuff up in the air. What do you think, Grandad?'

'I think it's lovely. Grand. Wasn't that lovely, Ma? I'm looking forward to it. And your Aunty Beryl's going to come and see it as well. Lovely. Really lovely. And did Santa call round this way last night?'

'Grandad!'

'And what did he bring you, Gillian?'

'Suede jacket.'

'Very nice.'

'Record tokens. Bubble bath. ten-colour biro. St Christopher. Selection Box. Manicure set.'

'My God. Don't they get some stuff these days? We used to

think we were lucky if we got a penny whistle. Or a whip and top. Didn't we, Ma? And your Dad. He never had a lot. In them days, anybody asked what they were getting for Christmas, you'd say a doll or a drum and a kick up the bum. Eh, Ma? What did you get, Eileen?'

'The usual.'

'What? Kick up the bum?'

'Pair of slippers. Wrong size.'

'Has he kept the ticket?'

'Doesn't matter. They know me in that shop anyway. I'm back there every year the same. It's getting to be a regular affair.'

'I reckon it's him that needs taking back. Eh? Rub him out. Draw him again. Eh, son? How come you always get her the wrong size?'

'I do it on purpose, just to annoy her. Do you want that Scotch freshened up?'

'Yeah. Wouldn't say No. Do you need a hand, Eileen? You look flustered.'

'No, I'm all right, Pop. I'm just waiting for Ron to stop faffing around and carve.'

'Ma? Another port?'

'Not for me. And don't give me too much of anything, Eileen. Just a little bit of meat and potatoes.'

'You'll have a glass of wine though, Ma?'

'No. Wine's too acid. You're chucking your money around, aren't you? Wine?'

'Stuffing, Ma?'

'No thank you. It lies too heavy.'

'Chipolata?'

'Go on then. Give me half.'

'I'll have her other half. And her veggies. And anything else she doesn't want.'

'And here she's been telling me you're off your food. She told me you never eat anything at home these days.'

'I do all right. I make my own arrangements.'

'Well how about making your own arrangements round this table? Ma, you go next to Gillian. Susan, on the stool. Then Pop. And me and Eileen on this end to be near the stove.'

The Glovers, Christmas 1962, elbow to elbow round a table that is too small even with the extra flap up. Turkey, chipolatas, sage and onion stuffing, bread sauce, roast potatoes, peas, carrots, sprouts and gravy, lapping the very edges of the plates. Eileen and Gillian on Tizer. Ron on Mateus *Rosé* with a little help from Susan. Pop still on Scotch. Ma making a meal of a slice of turkey and a small ruby port. And Gums, in perpetual optimistic motion, nudging his wet maw against each arm in turn, hustling shamelessly for meat.

'Got rid of your pouffe, son?'
　'Yeah.'
'Tell him. Go on.'
　'What?'
'Tell him what happened to the pouffe.'
　'Bloody thing.'
'He set light to it.'
　'In here?'
'No, he took it out the back. Shouting and swearing and carrying on.'
　'What for?'
'And kicking it. He kept kicking it. This is what I have to put up with. When he takes against something he goes loopy. Nobody knows.'
　'We'd have had it. We could have used it if you didn't want it any more. There wasn't anything wrong with it, was there?'
'Not a mark on it.'
　'We'd have had it.'
'And he keeps threatening my kitchen cabinet. He says it's ugly.'
　'It is bloody ugly. Christ, Eileen, give it a rest. It's Christmas afternoon.' *Christmas fucking afternoon and we're sitting here*

234

talking about kitchen cabinets. Too hot. That bastard fire's either roaring up the chimney or it's dead. Eileen's legs are turning red. Jack. Jack'll be stretched out on her beige settee, listening to Tony Bennett or opera or something. 'Ah, not the circus, Eileen.'

'There's nothing else.'

'Do you want a go with my Solitaire, Dad?'

'Maybe later, sweetheart.'

'Do you want to have a look at my *Girl* annual?'

'Yeah, later on.'

'Don't suppose you fancy a bit of a stroll, do you, son?'

Pop, leaning forward, making his proposition with a low voice and a meaningful look.

'Yeah, wouldn't mind. Eileen? Me and Pop are going to stretch out legs. Get a breath of air. You all right?'

'Yeah, we're watching the circus. Ma's asleep. Yeah, go on. Get out from under my feet. Make him wrap up warm though.'

Half-past three on Christmas afternoon. Nobody on the street except a black and tan dog with a tail that curls over its back, and Murgatroyd, too far away to speak, out with his granddaughter and her new doll's pram.

'I hate Christmas afternoon.'

'Me too, son.'

'I feel that cooped up.'

'Yes.'

'Jesus it's cold.' *Out walking with Pop. I don't do that. What do we talk about?* 'City had a good match Saturday.'

'Is there a phone box this way, son?'

'Yeah. Or the other way. What for? Ah. Right.'

'I told Beryl I'd try and give her a ring after dinner. See how she's going on. She's at her sister's.'

'Right.' *Say something. Ask him how far it's gone. He wants you to say something. It's not normal for Grandads to be phoning other women. Specially not on Christmas Day. He wants you to ask.*

235

'Been a nice bit of company for you, since she moved next door.'

'Champion. I tell you what, I wish she'd moved next door to me fifty years ago. It's a terrible thing, son, realizing what you missed.'

'You see her most days then?'

'See her every day. We do all sorts. If it's nice I might meet her up the rec and we'll have a little walk. Or if it's not so good we do a crossword. Listen to the wireless. All sorts.'

'How do you square it with Ma?'

'Don't have to. She thinks I'm round the bend anyway, so I just go out. She thinks I'm wandering. Going doolally. It's all right. All for the best. I've done my time with Ma. I don't wish her any harm, but I've done my whack. Mickey Rooney would have left her years ago.'

'You're not leaving her?'

'No. Mind, I live in hopes she'll leave me. I'm hoping she'll run off with one of them old wheezers down the Seniors. You'd better come in the box with me. You'll catch your death out there.'

'No, you don't want me listening in.'

'Don't be so daft. Come on. We can squeeze up.'

'. . . and I'm missing you, my darling. Yes, No. Yes, Eileen did us a lovely dinner, and I've been helping Ron with a bottle of Bell's. He's here with me in the phone box. Yes. Beryl says Merry Christmas . . .'

'Yeah.' *I could do that. He's levelled with me. I could level with him, man to man. No. Don't consider it. You could though. If Tony answers you can just hang up. If Jack answers, Tony'll ask her who it is. He might be round at Audrey's. No. Jack said. Christmas Day at home, then off up to Wetherby. Shooting and stuff. No. Forget it.*

'. . . all right, my darling. No, well, Ron's friend ran us this morning. He's got a little motor so we got took to the door, but we shall get a taxi home. Have a bit of tea and then make tracks. All right, my love. Miss you. Yeah. Miss you too.'

236

Pop, flushed with love and whisky, shining and twinkling in the falling light. Ronnie, no longer able to feel his feet, making a rash bid for camaraderie.

'Got any change left? I could do with making a call myself.' *No. Take it back.*

Too late. Too late to prevent hostility from thinning the air.

'Just a friend I said I might call. You know how it is?' *Idiot. He doesn't see any connection. He thinks what he's doing is all right. Dial the fucking number. Get it over with. No. Just say you changed your mind. Jack. I want to hear Jack and say Miss you, my love. Pop did. I want to.*

'What friend's that then, son?'

'Just, you know . . . ?'

Tony's voice, and the dogs faintly in the background.

'Hello? Hello? Audrey, is that you? Hello? Jack, are you expecting a call? Hello? One of your pieces of rough I think, pumpkin. Lost his tongue. Hello? Hello? Please yourself.'

'Wrong number.'

'Better try again.'

'No, I'll leave it. Try tomorrow.'

'As long as your friend's not expecting you. Not sitting waiting.'

'No.'

'We'll get back then? Get back to that fire?'

'Yeah.' *One of your pieces of rough, pumpkin.*

'Dinner was nice. Eileen did us proud.'

'Yeah.' *Here it comes. The standing fucking ovation for Eileen.*

'Great girl. Keeps things nice for you. And she's not afraid of hard graft. You've got a diamond there.'

'Yeah.'

'You're bound to have your ups and downs. Stands to reason. But she'd do anything for you and them girls. See, Ma never really wanted to go in for family life. I mean, you came along and she did her best, but she was never really cut out for it. She was happy

237

at Thornton's. And she made good money. She made more than me, you know? But Eileen's always put you and the kiddies first.'

Women like Eileen don't grow on trees. She's a diamond. She's twenty-four-carat gold with brass knobs on. Come on. Let's have the full SP, you hypocritical old bastard. The grass always looks greener. You never appreciate what you've got till it's gone. I do know what I've got. I've got a nice wife who reads Titbits *and fucks like a sack of spuds. And I've got a woman who holds me tight inside her and makes a cry that'd waken the dead, like the peacocks down the Abbey Park, and she doesn't care who bloody hears. And she knows about Leonardo da Vinci and stuff.* 'I tell you what Pop.'

'Yes?'

'You mind your own fucking business and I'll mind mine.'

Christmas tea, at least two hours too early because Ma is worried about the fog. Tinned pink salmon, ham with orange crumbs on the outside, cheese, lettuce, tomatoes and celery. Trifle with hundreds and thousands staining the custard, mince pies, chocolate covered marshmallows in red and silver paper, and iced fruit cake with a gold cardboard frill, a robin and three little men in top hats.

'What are the three little men again, Mum?'
  'The Town Waits.'
  'What are the Town Waits?'
  'They're traditional.'
  'Annette has a snowman on her cake.'
  'More tea, Pop? Ma? And help yourself to bread. I can easily spread some more.'

The meal proceeding in leaden silence, unresponsive to Eileen's pleasantness and *Top Cat* on the telly. Susan making a treble-decker sandwich of ham, tomato, cheese and salad cream. Ronnie brooding, the salmon turning to ash in his mouth. *One of your pieces of rough, pumpkin. Lost his tongue. One of your pieces of rough that's had you on the floor and up against the wall and even in your fur coat.* Ronnie, shifting in his seat to accommodate the all-time great of boners. Eileen mashing tea, spreading bread. Pop and Gillian, open-mouthed at *Daffy Duck*. And Ma, with her thin knuckly hand smoothing the tablecloth, looking puzzled.

'Oh, Archie, you do seem a long way away.'

Ma's cup of tea knocked over the best white cloth, and then Ron and Susan's long slow dance towards her, with Gums grumbling under the table and *Loony Tunes* playing on the telly.

'What's she say?'

'She said you seem a long way away, Grandad. Are you all right, Grandma?'

'Eileen? I don't think Ma's very well. Ma?'

'Loosen her clothes.'

'How do you mean?'

'Just loosen her clothes. That's what you have to do. Ma? Come on now. This is Eileen speaking. Ma? Do you want a glass of water? She's had too much port.'

'She's hardly had any port. She's a horrible colour, Eileen. Ma? Will you switch that fucking telly off, Gillian?'

'Pop, what do you think? Has she had a do like this before?'

Pop, silent, chewing, noncommittal.

'Should we phone the doctor?'

'Christmas night. You can't phone on Christmas night. He'll be having his tea. Ma? Come on, Ma. Let's get you to the kitchen door. Get a breath of air. Ron, get this tablecloth off and rinse it in the sink before it stains. Susan, stop that now. Thirteens don't cry.'

'I think Grandma's died, Mum. I can smell a smell.'

'Don't be stupid.'

240

'I can, Mum. I think she made a smell before she died. Gums thinks so. Look at him.'

'Susan, just shut up and let me think. Ma? Come on, Ma? Try and sit yourself up.'

'Eileen? I think Susan's right. I think she's gone. I'll get the doctor.'

'No, get an ambulance.'

'What for, if she's gone?'

'She might not have. What do you think, Pop? Doctor or ambulance?'

'Don't ask me. She's never been badly before.'

'I'll run down the phone box.'

'Tell them it's very urgent. Tell them she's an old lady and she's under Dr McKenzie. Tell them we're sorry to bother them on Christmas night.'

Ronnie Glover running to the telephone in his donkey jacket and his slippers, slowed down by dinner and tea and seventeen years of Eileen's cooking, but hurrying as best he can to get an ambulance for his mother who has already been dead five minutes.

One o'clock. Two o'clock. Three. Half-three. Not a wink.

'Eileen?'

'Yeah. You all right?'

'Can't sleep.'

'No.'

'Keep going over it.'

'Yeah.'

'Funny thing to say, wasn't it?'

'What?'

'Calling him Archie. She never called him Archie.'

'No. He should have stopped here. Gillian could have had the settee.'

'He'll be all right. I'll go round first thing.' *He'll be all right.*

You're not leaving her, are you? No, I'm hoping she'll leave me. One of your pieces of rough, pumpkin. Jack. Going off in the morning. Shan't be able to tell her. Can't do anything. Go for a stroll with her or anything. Pop can. With Beryl. He can now. You can't. What a stupid fucking set-up. All this ducking and diving for a bit of whassisname, and thinking about it all the time. Thirty-eight and thinking about that all the time. Sitting there with a stiffy at Christmas tea and your Ma slipping away. Hell, Ma, what happens? You watch a bit of circus, have a little bit of ham and half a cup of tea. Then you say Oh Archie. What a stupid bloody thing to say. What a stupid bloody woman. I was back at Thornton's before you were three weeks old. He was that slow and stupid your Pop. Nobody knows what I have to put up with. We have to manage on the pension, you know. You're chucking your money around, aren't you? Wine? Make that Vimto last. Go straight home. If you don't . . .

'Ron?'

'Yeah?'

'I was just thinking, if they'd come and put that flipping telephone in, we could have got an ambulance here faster.'

'Yeah. Wouldn't have made any odds though. She'd gone anyway. They said.'

'Yeah.'

'I wonder where you go? Do you think you just wake up somewhere else? Do you think it's like when you get to a boarding house and somebody has to show you where the lav is and tell you what time for dinner?'

'Well they reckon there's people waiting for you, don't they?'

'What, like Jesus and that?'

'No, you know, ones who've passed over before you.'

'Who reckons that?'

'It's just what people reckon. They say there's a bright light and then you see all your loved ones waiting for you at like a gate, leading into a beautiful garden.'

'So she probably thinks she's down the Abbey Park?'

'Yeah.'

'What loved ones? She hasn't got any loved ones. She fell out with everybody.'

'There'd be somebody there to meet her. How about her Mum and Dad?'

'No. She fell out with them. And that's another thing. I mean, if you're ignorant and quarrelsome and you go round scrapping with everybody here, do you just carry on the same up there? I bet you do. There's probably some poor bastard in his new billet tonight, thinks he's landed on his feet, and he doesn't realize he's got Ma for all fucking eternity. Perhaps you can put in for a swap? Like a council-house exchange. Do you think, Eileen? Eileen?'

Ronnie, as wide awake as a man can be, trying to get a picture of his Ma inside his head and not being able to, not being able to remember her face at all even though he was sitting opposite her at teatime, watching her dentures slip and slide.

'Dear oh dear. Well I am sorry. What a thing. She looked right enough that morning. I mean your Dad sat in the front with me and he had plenty to say. She was quiet. But she looked right enough. Just shows, don't it? So how's he going on?'

'He's all right. His lady friend came rushing back and he's round there most of the time. Eileen says it'll really hit him after the funeral, but I don't think so. They never got on.'

'Yeah, but that's sometimes the worst. Jean's Mam and Dad, they had two little terriers, little Westies, and they hated the sights of one another. You couldn't leave them in a room together. Any road, one of them got a growth and she had to be put down, and the other one just pined away. Wouldn't eat anything and just faded away. Nobody to scrap with, see?'

'Well Pop's not fading away. Beryl's making him hotpots. And ironing his pyjamas.'

'When's the funeral?'

'Friday. Crematorium.'

'Are you having people back?'

'Yeah. Back at Pop's. Eileen and Beryl are wrestling one another over who's making the sandwiches. Mind, there's hardly going to be anybody. When you think about it, who is there? A few old dears from the Seniors' Club and us. That's it. Anyway, how was your Christmas?'

'Very nice. I put a little wrought-iron shelf up for Jean's Toby jugs. Looks smashing. Here, and guess who I saw Christmas night when I was taking our old lady home?'

'What?'

'Pearce.'

'Yeah?'

'With a girl.'

'Never.'

'Got his arm round her.'

'Never in this world.'

'I'm telling you. Ask him.'

'I shall. Anyway, Vic, it's Friday morning at eleven o'clock. So I'll come in for the afternoon.'

'You'll do no such thing. You won't feel like work. And there'll be stuff needs doing, won't there? Clearing her stuff?'

'Eileen's made a start on that. I think she's been a bit quick off the mark, you know? Bloody hell. One minute you're going along, right as ninepence. Next thing there's nothing left of you and all your coats and woollies are on the way to the jumble. But here's a funny thing. Eileen said she'd make a start on the big sideboard. Ma had it stacked with blouses and cardies and stuff, and a box with old photos and birthday cards. She'd got stuff that went back years. All clean and tidy. Anyway Eileen opens the sideboard. Nothing there. Well, about two jumpers. Everything else was gone.'

'Somebody been in and helped themselves?'

'No. That's the thing. Nobody's been in, only Pop. All gone. Eileen reckons she must have had a feeling, you know? Tidied things up while she could.'

'Had a premonition, like?'

245

'Yeah. I'm cross about the box of photos though. I'd have liked to have had them. So the only picture we've got of her is our wedding group. And here's another funny thing. I can't remember what she looked like.'

'Kiddies all right?'

'Yeah. Susan keeps going on about it. What happens if your heart stops. What happens if your brain stops. She's not upset. I thought she would be. Gillian, I don't know. She's not said a word. She went upstairs out of the way while we were waiting for the ambulance, and she's not said a word. We're getting the phone on Monday.'

'Smashing. And don't forget, you take all day Friday. You'll still get paid.'

'Cheers, Vic.'

Ronnie Glover, planning to sing properly at his Ma's funeral instead of just mouthing like he did at Uncle Nev's. And say nice things about her to Pop, and be pals and help clear up, and then go for a bike ride down Gartree Road on Friday afternoon to see if there's any signs of life at Jack's.

Eileen and Ronnie. Pop, Mrs Orr from Seniors and the lady that does their teas, Aunty Ivy from Kidderminster, Jean Shires, and the two Miss Woods who used to be neighbours when they lived in Faraday Street and saw the notice because they always read the Births, Marriages & Deaths. And a vicar. Pop called him the chaplain. Aunty Ivy called him the parson. Nobody knew him from Adam and he called Ma Dorothy. Pop, sitting there dry-eyed, like he was at the wrong funeral, thinking about Beryl probably, back at Glebe Crescent in her frilly apron, cutting sandwiches for the grieving hordes.

The Twenty-third Psalm, the only one they could think of when the man from the Co-op asked them to choose, croaked and whispered to a relieved conclusion. Ronnie, fidgeting in his suit, leafing through the Book of Common Prayer, trying to imagine Ma stretched out inside that box.

The Churching of Women. The Woman, at the usual time after her delivery, shall come into the church decently apparelled . . . To Be Used At Sea. Special Prayers with respect to the Enemy. Short

Prayers in respect of a Storm. Has she still got that brown dress on? Or do they put you in a nightie or something? Somebody said Uncle Nev was in his best suit and Ma said it was a waste. I should have gone to see her. Somebody should've. I wonder if her Christmas dinner's still in her stomach. They found an Ancient Briton in a peat bog and they could tell what he'd been eating just before he died . . .

'Ron.'

'What?'

'Stand up.'

'Sorry.'

'Ron.'

'What?'

'Are we supposed to ask the vicar back? Afterwards.'

'Don't know.' *O teach us to number our days that we may apply our hearts unto wisdom. Don't want people hanging around for hours saying how fucking marvellous she was. I want to get off round Jack's. See if she's back. Don't want Pop getting stuck into the Scotch neither. He might say something.* 'Eileen?'

'What?'

'No need to invite him. The people at the Co-op said they were booked through solid all day. They've got a backlog because of Christmas.'

'All right.'

When I go I'd like a really good send-off. Plenty of grub and nice wine and dancing and everything. Everybody says that. They still end up with boiled ham and the Twenty-third fucking Psalm. 'Eileen.'

'What?'

'It was nice of Jean to come.'

'Ssh.'

Friday afternoon. The Ponderosa, all in darkness.

What did she say? Going to Wetherby on Boxing Day for about a week. How long is about a week? They might be stuck up there, if they've had snow. Wetherby's . . . up there somewhere. Ah Jack, how am I supposed to know? You left it all up in the air. You never said when to come round again. Panto rehearsals. Susan'll know when you're due back. Yeah.

Ronnie, unsettled because his Ma just died and now she's not there to annoy him, and because Jack's away, some place he doesn't know, till some time he doesn't know, and he ought to ask Eileen for sex, it being Friday, otherwise she might smell a rat. Ronnie, who can't be bothered to do any drawing, or get his Italian book out, even though he's got nearly a whole afternoon free and man that is born of woman hath but a short time to live.

'I wasn't sure what to do. Whether to come round or phone up or what. We're on the phone now.'

'Did you phone on Christmas Day?'

Say No. 'Yes.'

'That wasn't very bright.'

'Just wanted to say Merry Christmas.'

'We'd already done that.'

'How was Wetherby?'

'Fine. Lovely.'

'How's the panto coming along?'

'Fine. Still lots to do though. I'm just on my way out to see the pianist actually.'

'And you? You all right?' *Give me a sign, Jack. Touch me. Crack a joke. Don't make me ask.*

'Yes, I'm fine. What's eating you?'

'Nothing.'

'You've not told your wife or anything stupid?'

'No. Nothing. My mother died. Christmas Day.'

'I'm sorry.'

'Yeah, well. You've got a lot to do. I'd better let you get off.'
When am I going to see you, Jack? It's not just the whassisname. I want to see you. I want everything to be all right between us.

'Yes, I must go. You'll be coming to see Susan in the show?'

'Yes, Eileen's got tickets for us.'

'Good. Well. Nice to see you. Sorry to hear about your mother. And I'll be in touch when we're ready to have the bedroom done.'

'Yeah, OK. Shall I give you the phone number?'

'Good idea. I'll put it in my book.'

It's finished, Glover. She's switched off. It was that stupid bloody phone call. She thinks you're going to do something daft and blow the gaff. You're finished. You did her a drawing and she fucked you wearing her fur coat and now she's switched off. Look what she's written next to your number. Decorator. Not Ron. Fucking decorator.

Jacqueline Granger, fussing with car keys, pulling up her collar, moving towards the door with Ronnie's heart in her hands.

'Cheer up. It may never happen.'

'Yeah.'

Jack, pushing his specs up his nose and kissing him gently on the side of his face.

'Happy New Year.'

Yeah! She's all right. We're all right. I was imagining it. She's just got a lot on her mind. The panto and everything. Ah, God. What a bloody relief. Nearly blew it. Nearly said something. All right now though. Guts have stopped churning. Can go home now. Have chips and egg. Get the Italian books out. Do it with Eileen on the roller towel. Brilliant.

'And to you, Jack. A very happy new year.'

251

'Can't somebody else do it tonight? I sat on my own the other night.'

'You won't be sitting on your own tonight. You'll have Pop and Beryl and Gillian.'

'But don't you want to sit and watch it?'

'I've heard it from the back that many times it's getting on my pippin. And anyway, they need me to help dress the little ones. It's bedlam back there, Ron. Every minute there's one of them lost her shoes or needs the toilet or something. And I've promised Madame.'

Promised Madame. Big mates with Madame all of a sudden. 'Well I feel a bit of a pillock sat there without you.'

'Ah, go on. You'll enjoy it. And be nice to Pop. I've told Susan she can stay for half an hour afterwards but that's all.'

'What do you mean? Stay?'

'For the party afterwards. Because it's the last night. I did tell you, Ron. It's more for the grown-ups really, so I said half an hour, one glass of Pepsi and then home. I'll stop with her. Madame said to.'

'So what am I supposed to do?'

'Take Gillian home.'

'Can't we come to the party?'

'No. It's for cast and helpers.'

'I painted some scenery.'

'For about five minutes from what I heard. Young Raymond's done a lot of it.'

'Oh well then.'

'So you take Gillian home and we'll be along after. You could get chips.'

'Bloody panto.' *Everybody's fixed up. Pop's with Beryl. Gillian's got another lad. Susan and Eileen are invited to this party. And Pearce, only he's Raymond all of a sudden and he's fixed up with that girl with the big legs. Prince Charming. Jack's busy. Running round. Black trousers. Black jumper. Busy with the dancers and the band. Having a laugh with that bloke who's got the clipboard. Try and catch her eye. No. Chat to Beryl.* 'How do you think Pop's doing?'

'He's all right. I shan't let him come to any harm.'

'No.'

'He talks about your Ma, you know?'

'Does he?'

'Talks about her a lot. I did when I lost my husband. You go back over all the little things, over and over, and then one morning you wake up and you're ready for something new. Doesn't matter if you were happy or not. You still have to do it. Have another toffee?'

Two and a half hours of forgotten lines and dancers like elephants. Susan, suddenly too big for a fairy, gazing round for her Grandad. Annette's Dad showing off on the front row with a flash camera. Tony, in a suit, double-vent jacket, sharp haircut, sauntering round like Lord of the Manor. And Pearce, in a warehouse coat, sweeping the stage at half-time, him and another bloke, doing it to something from *Swan Lake*, dancing with their brooms, bringing the house down.

'Highlight of the show.'
   I could have done that. If they'd asked me.

Ronnie, in a monkey mood, wishing to be invisible *and* the most important man in the hall. Fiddling with his sleeves. Trying to rub the toffee feeling off his teeth with his tongue. Pretending to listen to Beryl, but aware, every single moment, of Jack.

*G*o out, Eileen. Go round Pop's and see if he's all right. Just let me have five minutes alone with this telephone. 'Fancy a bit of choccy?'

'We haven't got any.'

'You could fetch some. Gibson's are still open.'

'No. It's horrible out. It's all gone to slush.'

'A bit of choccy'd be nice though.'

'You go if you're so keen.'

'Ah Eileen, go on. I'm knackered.'

'Have a tangerine.'

'I want choccy.'

'I must be mad.'

'No, you're lovely.' *Clear off. Leave me alone with this phone. If I don't talk to Jack I shall bust.*

'What do you want?'

'Fruit & Nut. Bring something for the girls as well. Bring some crisps.'

*   *   *

'Where's Mum?'

'Gone to Gibson's. Haven't you got homework?'

'Finished it. Who were you phoning?'

Susan Glover, appearing in the doorway the very instant Ronnie had started to dial.

'Nobody. Aunty Beryl. Thought I might give her a call, but I'll go round tomorrow. See how your Grandad's doing.'

Be in, Jack. Be in, be alone, be awake. Please. 'Jack?'

'Hello?'

'Jack?'

'I can hardly hear you. Who is it?'

'It's Ron. Jack?'

'Do you know what time it is?'

'Sorry. I had to wait till everybody was asleep. I just wanted to speak to you.'

'What would you have done if Tony had been here?'

'Hung up.'

'I thought you'd got more sense.'

'I'm sorry. I've missed you.'

'I'll phone you. Tomorrow.'

'Yeah. Ask me round to price a job. Have you decided about the bedroom?'

'For Christ's sake, Ron, it's the middle of the night. I'll phone you.'

'Tomorrow?'

'Probably.'

T en past eight.

Phone me, Jack. Phone and ask me round. Now. She's walking to her phone. She's dialling the number. It's going to ring. Now. Now, you bastard telephone. Ring.

Twelve minutes past eight.

Watch telly. Read something. Next thing you know, it'll be ringing. Hello, my love. Can you come straight round?

Thirteen minutes past eight.

'Whatever is wrong with you?'

'Nothing.'

'I shall be glad when it's warm enough for you to go down the shed. Pacing around here. Take the dog out.'

'He doesn't want to go out.'

'Course he does. Dogs always want to go out.'

'I might bike round to Pop's.'

'He won't be there.'

'I mean bike round to Beryl's. See how he's doing.'

'Please yourself. Just stop pacing up and down here.'

The Ponderosa, eight thirty-five. Tony's car outside, looking like it's not going anywhere, looking like a dead good reason why Jack wouldn't have phoned the real man in her life.

'Beryl? You got Pop in there?'

'I have. He's snug as a bug in a rug with his crossword. Come on in. Archie? Young man here to see you.'

'Son? Obsolete coin, seven letters.'

'Cherry brandy, Ron?'

'Yeah, thanks.'

'Or a Grand Marnier? Or a Gaelic? I could do us all a nice Gaelic?'

'Yeah, anything. I don't mind. You all right, Pop?'

'Champion. Large bird, six letters. Third letter's N.'

'Eileen says are you going to come round for your tea one night?'

'What for?'

'Have your tea with us.'

'I have my tea with Beryl.'

'Right.'

'Little sandwich, Ron?'

'Not for me. I hope he's not wearing his welcome out.'

'Leave him alone. He's lovely. I like to have somebody to look after. The days are too long when you're on your own, but if you've got a man you've got a full-time job. Are you sure you won't have a little sandwich? I'm doing one for Archie.'

'Kiddies all right, son?'

'Yeah.' *Kiddies all right. Kiddies. You never bothered if this kiddy was all right, out on the step with a bottle of Vimto. Didn't matter what she did, you never said a word. She made me stop off school with you when you had shingles, so she could go to work. You never stood up to her. You were a gutless bloody wonder, you smug overfed bastard.*

258

'Adelaide match looks like it's in the bag.'
'Yep.'

Go home. Fetch dog. Walk him towards the golf-course. Just happen to see her walking the poodles. Got to talk to you, Jack. No, not GOT TO. Casual. Fancy seeing you here. Love you, Jack. I won't be any bother to you. Just want to see you sometimes. Once a week. Once a month. Do it quick. Might miss her if you're not really fast. When you try to make your legs go faster, they go slower. Sometimes you don't move at all.

The Ponderosa, nine fifty-five. Tony and Jacqueline Granger's cars parked for the night, side by side, and a man on a bike labouring past, losing ground to six white horses with big laughing mouths and riders with no faces at all.

'Come on then, dog, if you're coming.'
  'Ron? Where have you been?'
  'Pop's. Beryl's. And now I'm taking the dog out.'
  'He's been out. He's settled now.'
  'You said dogs always want to go out, so he can just come out again.'
  'What's the matter with you? In and out, in and out. You can get your Italian book out if you want. I shan't mind.'
  'Eileen, shut up. Gums, get out here now.'

Eileen, face set, going back to her film. Gums, stretching and scratching, leaving his fireside for something that sounds promising. Ronnie, taking three goes to slam the door because the damp weather has made the wood swell, then gone into the night, a man and his dog.

'Madame phoned. Says she won't be having her bedroom done after all. And somebody called Markham. Says you're supposed to be doing a ceiling for him. Ron?'

Gutless. Doing crosswords in his slippers. Kiddies all right, son? Letting her take your razor strop to me. Never answered her back till she was an old lady. Fixed up with Beryl. Little sandwich, Archie? Bastard. Bastard.

Chucking-out time at the Three Blackbirds, the Boot and the Cadogan Arms. Headlights swinging out of car parks and men made invincible by drink, barrelling home through fine heavy rain, careless of a black and tan mongrel who has smelled the scent of love. Just a glancing blow. No blood. No noise. Just the swish of traffic, and Ronnie Glover, staggering home with the best dog in the world, trying to keep him dry and warm, trying to hold up a head that's hanging all wrong.

'I'm sorry, Eileen. I'm sorry. I don't know how it happened.'

'I thought I mind find you in here. Are you in a bad way?'

Vic Shires, looking in on his mate Ronnie Glover, who hasn't shown up for work or sent a message, and isn't answering the phone because he's sitting in his shed on a fishing stool, frozen to the marrow, eyes closed up with crying.

'What's up, chap? Is it about your Mam? What? What is it? Oh dear God. The poor little bugger. What happened? Car hit him? He's as stiff as a board. How long have you had him out here? Ron? What are you going to do with him? We'll have to do something with him. Do you want a hand? I could run you round the vet's. They'll know what to do. I mean, no point trying to bury him here. The ground's like iron. Eh? Shall we run him round the vet's? Ah mate, don't take on. He was a smashing little dog, but these things happen. He had a good life, didn't he? You told me yourself. Plenty of grub. Plenty of how's-your-father. And I don't suppose he knew what hit him. Out like a light. Ron?'

261

Ronnie, sobbing from the depths of his aching chest, tears dripping from his chin, top lip glistening, words juddering and stalling.

'Gums.'

'Yeah, mate.'

'My fault.'

'These things happen, Ron.'

'Should have . . . lead. Should have. Sorry. Best mate. Best dog. Never should have . . .'

'Now come on. Blow your nose and we'll put him in the back of my motor.'

'Everything's gone bad.'

'Has it?'

'I've done a terrible terrible thing and everything's gone bad. I've been horrible to Eileen. And now this. My little dog. Don't want him to be dead, Vic. I want to make him all right again.'

'Come up the house and have a cup of tea. I'm frozen so you must be.'

'I've been having relations. I've been having another woman. Up Gartree Road. And now she's finished it and I don't know why. We were great, me and Jack. And then she just finished it. She went on at me to get a phone put in and now I've got one she's never rung me. I can't think straight, Vic. I can't settle. After Jack, everything here's horrible. And now I've lost my best mate. He loved me, that little dog did.'

'You haven't told Eileen?'

'Course not.'

'You're an idiot, Glover.'

'Eileen doesn't know.'

'Women always know. She probably just hasn't realized she knows. She's a diamond, Eileen. One in a million.'

'I know all that. But she gets on my nerves. She's always yapping on about nothing. Looking at her catalogues. She's holding me back.'

262

'Holding you back from the loony bin. You're a tosser, Glover. She keeps everything nice for you. Looks after you and the girls. What's she meant to do, eh, go on the bloody Brains Trust? What does she stop you doing? You do your bits of drawing, she likes her telly. Fair enough. No reason to go off shagging some bony old mare with a posh voice.'

'What do you mean? Old mare?'

'Well.'

'She was beautiful to me, talking and that. It wasn't just shagging. She gave me a painting.'

'I don't want to hear about it. I wish you'd never told me. Now let's put that poor old boy on my back seat and get shot of him before he starts to pong.'

'He was my pal, Vic. Always went mad when he heard me open the gate.'

'Yeah.'

'What am I going to do?'

'Where's the vet?'

'Don't know. Near the Tigers' ground.'

'Right. Wipe your face and let's get round there. You know what you need? A little project. Something to keep you occupied. How about kitchen units? That's what I did when Jean had her hysterectomy. Fitted cupboards with a nice Formica top. Eileen'd like that. And I could give you a hand.'

'**D**o you really think this'll be all right?'

Eileen Glover, talking through a mouthful of pins as she lays out a paper pattern for her cap-sleeved boat-neck classic sheath in navy with a small white spot.

'Yes.'
Ronnie, off dresses, women, food, everything.

'Jean's bought something with an ecru lace trim and a little brocade jacket.'
'Yeah well, it's her party. She's got more cause to get dolled up.'
'You should get a new suit.'
'Waste of money.'
'Or a new shirt. I've been really looking forward to this and now you've got the hump. You haven't showed me the foxtrot or anything.'

264

'Can't remember it.'

'I shall go without you if you carry on like this.'

'Good.'

'That was the door.'

'I didn't hear anything.'

'It was. It was the back door.'

'If it was, they'll knock again.'

'Ron! I'm pinning my pattern and you're doing nothing. Just get out of that chair and see who it is.'

'Bollocks.'

'Is it all right if we come in? We did knock?'

Raymond Pearce, runt of the litter, rising star of the Dog & Gun Sunday XI and talk of the town since the final performance of *Cinderella*.

'This is Erica. She was Prince Charming.'

'Hello, Raymond. Fancy you coming round. Ron, look who's come round.'

'Only we've brought you something. I asked Vic and he said it was a good idea. Something to cheer you up. Erica's got it inside her coat.'

Prince Charming, with a spotty chin and a shy, pretty smile, opening her zipper just enough to show black ears and a ginger, worried brow instantly alert from a deep puppy sleep.

'Oh, Ron, look. He's lovely. Where's he from?'

'Erica's Mum's Brandy. She's had five. We thought you could have this one. After what happened.'

'Oh I don't know, Raymond. We haven't said we'll have another dog. See, I'm out at work now. When we got Gums the girls were still little. I was at home all day. I don't know. It was lovely of you to think of us, wasn't it, Ron? So you're courting now?'

Pearce, pink and pleased.

'Yes. Erica's going to come and help with teas when the cricket starts.'

'That's a nice thing to do. I wish our Gillian would do something like that.'

'Do you think you'd like to have him, Mrs Glover? He's trained. Nearly.'

'I don't know. I think it's a bit soon. And we got rid of everything. His water bowl and everything. Chucked it all out so it didn't keep reminding us. What do you think, Ron?'

Ronnie Glover, taking delivery of a saggy bag of loose furry skin and big soft feet, burying his nose into its sawdust smell, then looking again at the ridiculous prick of the ears.

No doubt about it. I'd know those ears anywhere. I knew your Dad. Knew him well. 'I'll buy him a water bowl on my way home from work. It's what Gums would have wanted.'

'I'll have your gâteau if you're not bothered.'

'Yeah.'

'It's dropped off you since Christmas, you know. I bet you've lost a stone. Have you weighed yourself?'

'No.'

'Do you feel all right?'

'Yes.'

'Well I wish I could lose it like that. This roll-on's cutting me in half. Jean looks nice. Do you think we'll manage twenty-five? We should have a do, like this. Melon and everything. Are you going to show me this dancing then?'

This is it. This is your punishment. 'Just feel the rhythm and follow me. See, if I press my left leg forward, you'll follow back with your right leg. You'll have to stand closer than that, Eileen. OK, back with your right, back with your left, side right, close left, feel the rhythm, forward right, forward left, side right, close left, quicker though. This is the quickstep. And just little steps. We haven't got the Albert Hall to get round. Don't stop and act daft when you make a mistake. Carry on. Just walk it through. Walk to the rhythm, Eileen.'

'You've picked it up fast. She must have given you more than one lesson.'

'No. Just a couple of goes. It's not hard. I don't know any of the fancy bits.'

'Well I'm very impressed. And I'm glad you've bucked up a bit. I had been thinking I might take you back, see if I could get a refund.'

'Yeah?'

'Yeah.'

'Sorry.' *Too much eye-shadow, Eileen. And you can see where that roll-on's digging in. Marshmallow thighs. You can see where you're bulging over your stocking tops. I don't really want to dance up against it, but I will do. That's my punishment. Make the best of a bad job.*

> *On State Street*
> *That great street*
> *I just wanna say*
> *They do things they never do on Broadway.*
> *They have the time, the time of their life*
> *I saw a man and he danced with his wife*
> *In Chicago, Chicago, my home town.*

'All right, Glover? Can I have a dance with your bird later on? You can have one with my old boiler. I'm keeping her on, did I tell you? Renewing her contract for another twelve months. Here, Glover, don't bother about a taxi. Jean's brother's going your way.'

Vic Shires, tootling past, easy and practised, with Jean in his arms, addressing Ronnie with a long old-fashioned look.

Yeah, yeah, yeah.

'And how's that little puppy dog? You tell him his Uncle Vic's going to come and take him to Bradgate Park one of these Sundays. Obedience training.'

Almost midnight. Bowling home in an Austin Healey, squashed up in the back behind Jean's brother who never married.

He could have gone left there. Would have been just as quick. Now he'll go down Gartree Road. Punishment.

'Oh look, Ron. Madame's bungalow's up for sale. I'd heard something was going on. According to Annette's Mum there's a lot of money owing. Bang go the dancing classes. I knew those shoes'd be a waste of money.'

Say something ordinary. 'Do you fancy a fish pond? I could do it in a weekend, once the weather's better.'

'And she has men. A lot of people have told me that. Over fifty and having men.'

Think of good things to do. Plan good things to do, then the pain gets less. That's the way it works. Dig a pond. Get driving lessons. One of your pieces of rough, pumpkin.

'Annette's Mum's sister used to do her cleaning and one time she found a pair of knickers behind the settee. Used. Man mad. She must be.'

Dig a pond. Get driving lessons. Train Bones to sit at the kerb and not cross over till he's told. Read The Cruel Sea.

'Could I trouble you to give the back window a wipe?'

Ronnie Glover, cleaning the rear windscreen with a nice clean duster, looking back down Gartree Road. An estate agent's board, receding fast. But neither sight nor sound of any horses.